BEAN and NUGGET

The Ball

Charise Mericle Harper

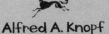

Alfred A. Knopf

THIS IS A BORZOI BOOK PUBLISHED BY ALFRED A. KNOPF

Published in the United States by Alfred A. Knopf, an imprint of Random House Children's Books, a division of Random House, Inc., New York.
Knopf, Borzoi Books, and the colophon are registered trademarks of Random House, Inc.
Visit us on the Web! randomhouse.com/kids
Educators and librarians, for a variety of teaching tools, visit us at RHTeachersLibrarians.com
Library of Congress Cataloging-in-Publication Data
Harper, Charise Mericle.
Bean Dog and Nugget : the ball / Charise Mericle Harper. — 1st ed.
p. cm.— (Bean Dog and Nugget)
Summary: Bean Dog and Nugget lose Bean Dog's shiny new ball in a bush.
They dream up elaborate and silly ways to get it back while they argue
about who is actually going to go and get it.
ISBN 978-0-307-97707-6 (pbk.) — ISBN 978-0-307-97708-3 (lib. bdg.) — ISBN 978-0-307-97709-0 (ebook)
1. Graphic novels. [1. Graphic novels. 2. Lost and found possessions—Fiction.
3. Friendship—Fiction. 4. Humorous stories.] I. Title.
PZ7.7.H37Beb 2013
741.5 973—dc23
2012029373

The text of this book is set in 16-point Matt Md Text.
The illustrations were created using digital coloring.

MANUFACTURED IN MALAYSIA
May 2013 10 9 8 7 6 5 4 3 2 1 First Edition

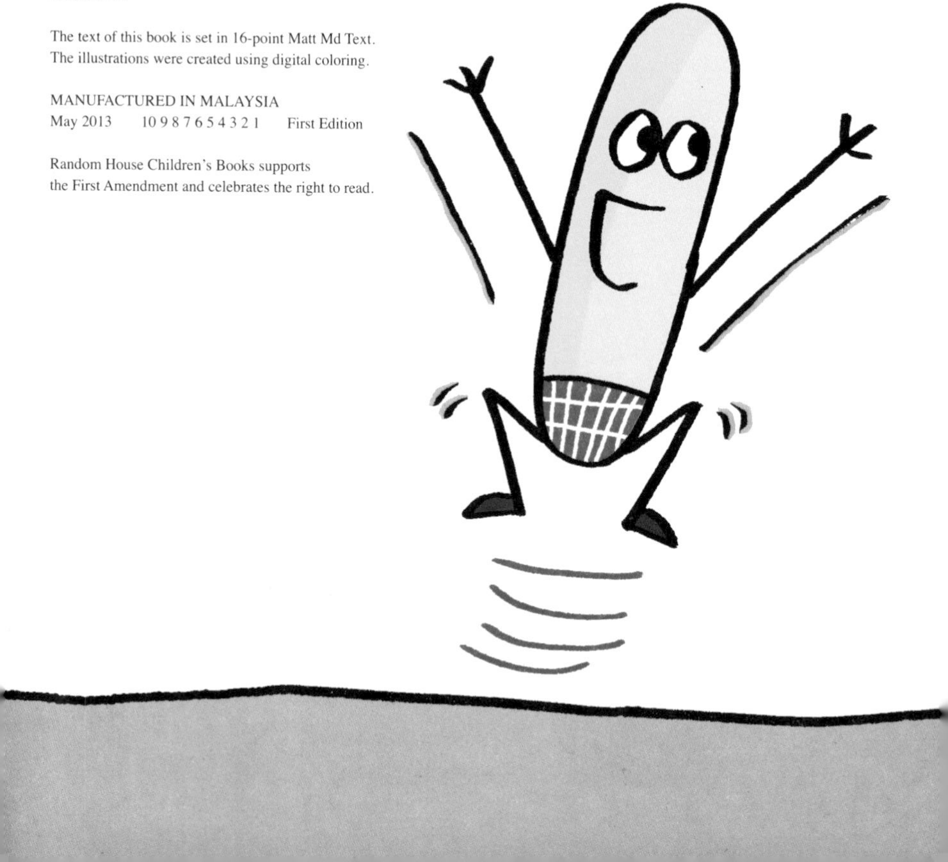

For Luther and Cole,
two great boys

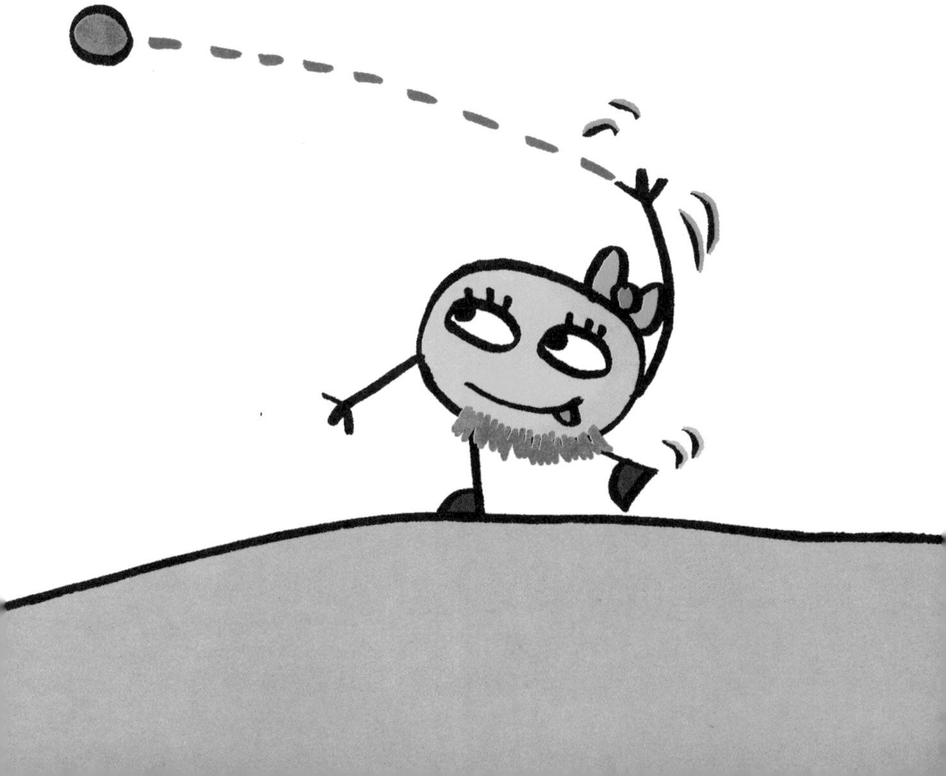

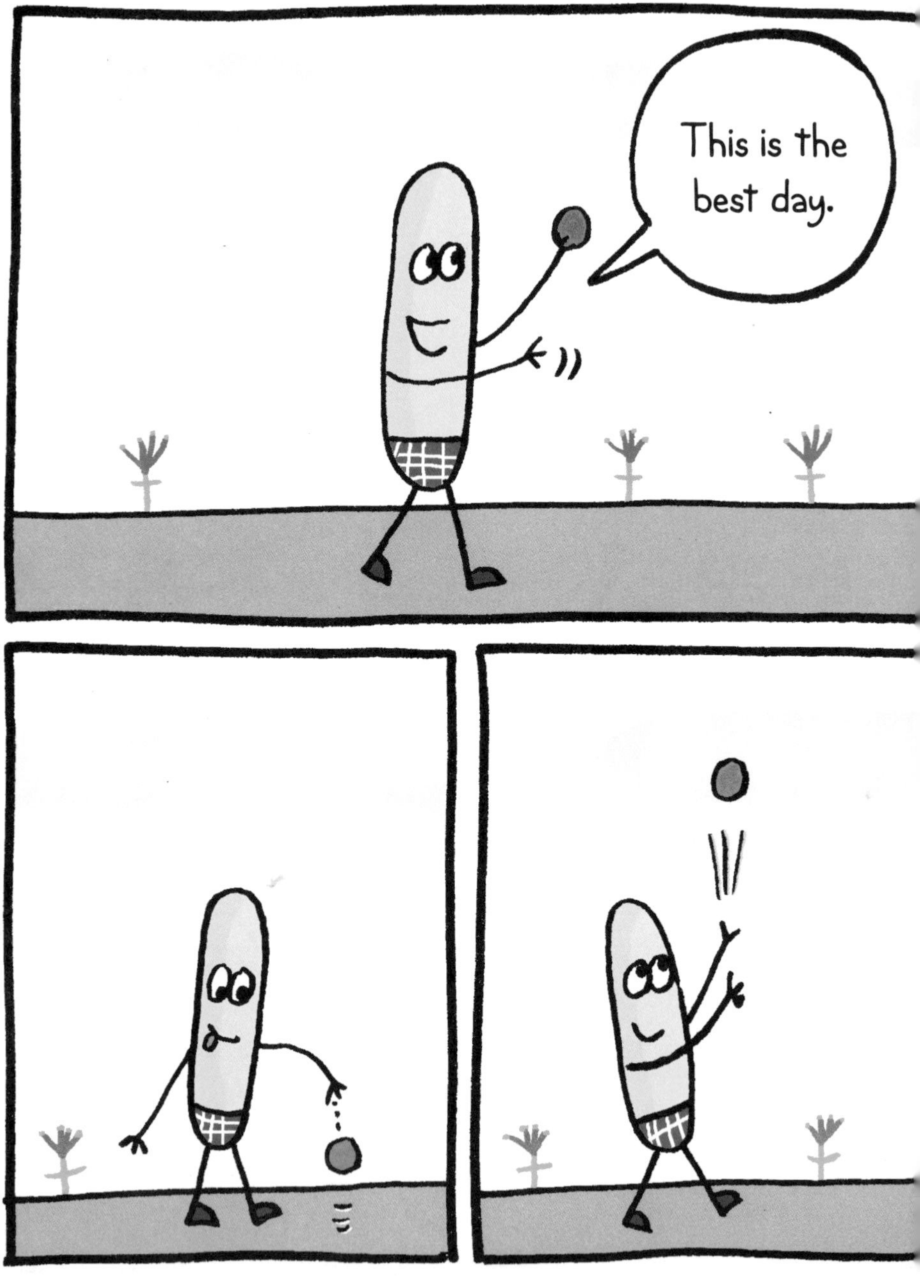
This is the best day.

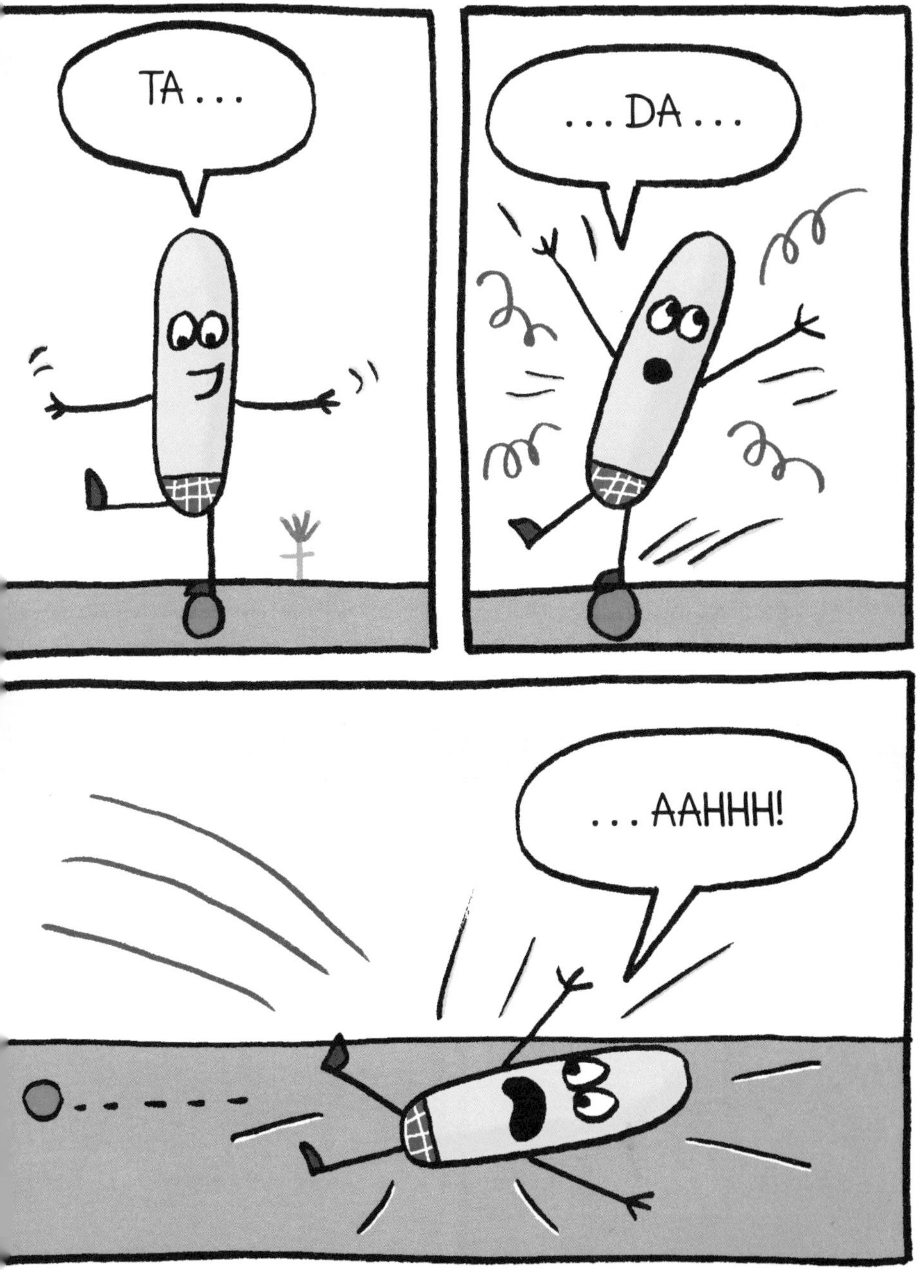
TA . . .
. . . DA . . .
. . . AAHHH!

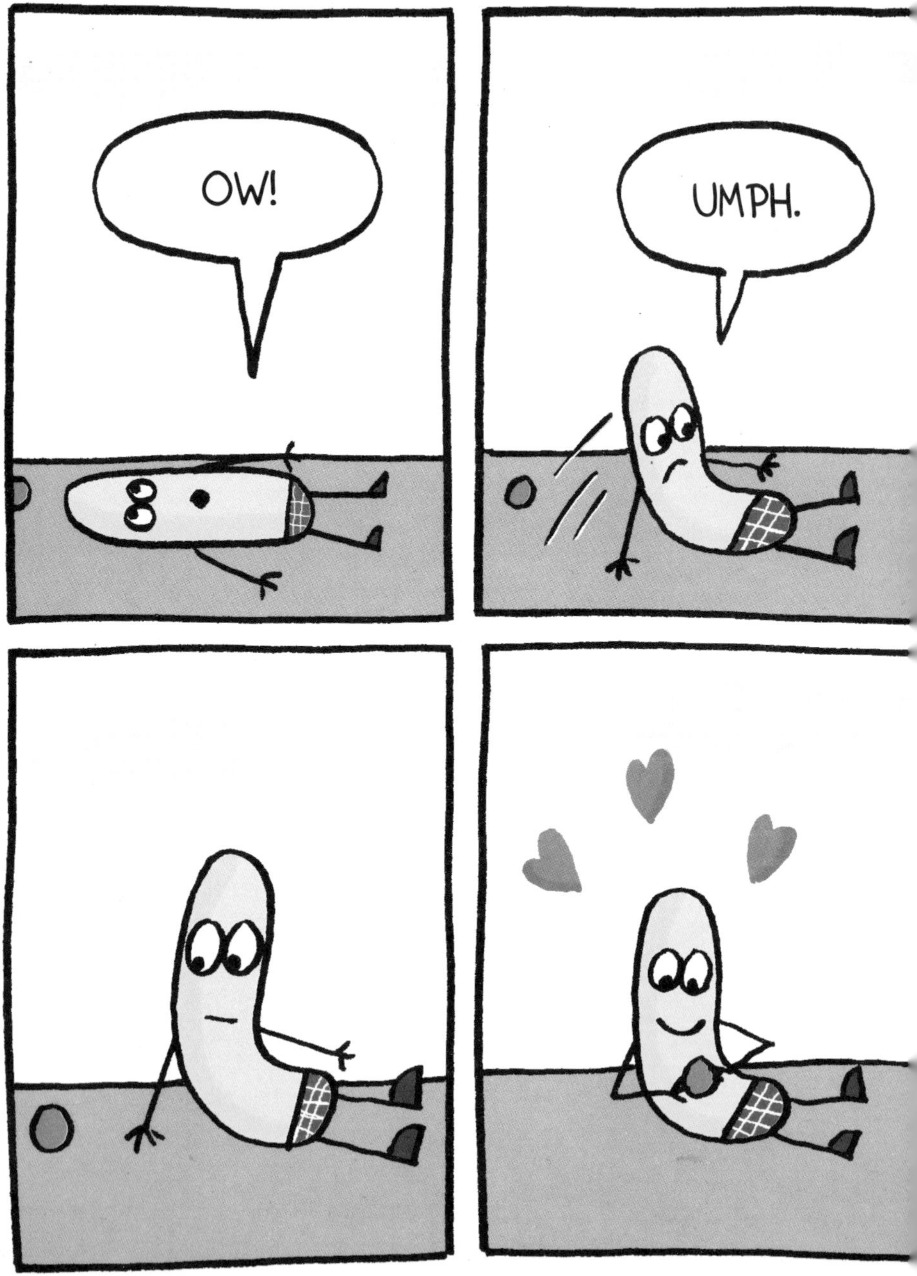
OW!
UMPH.

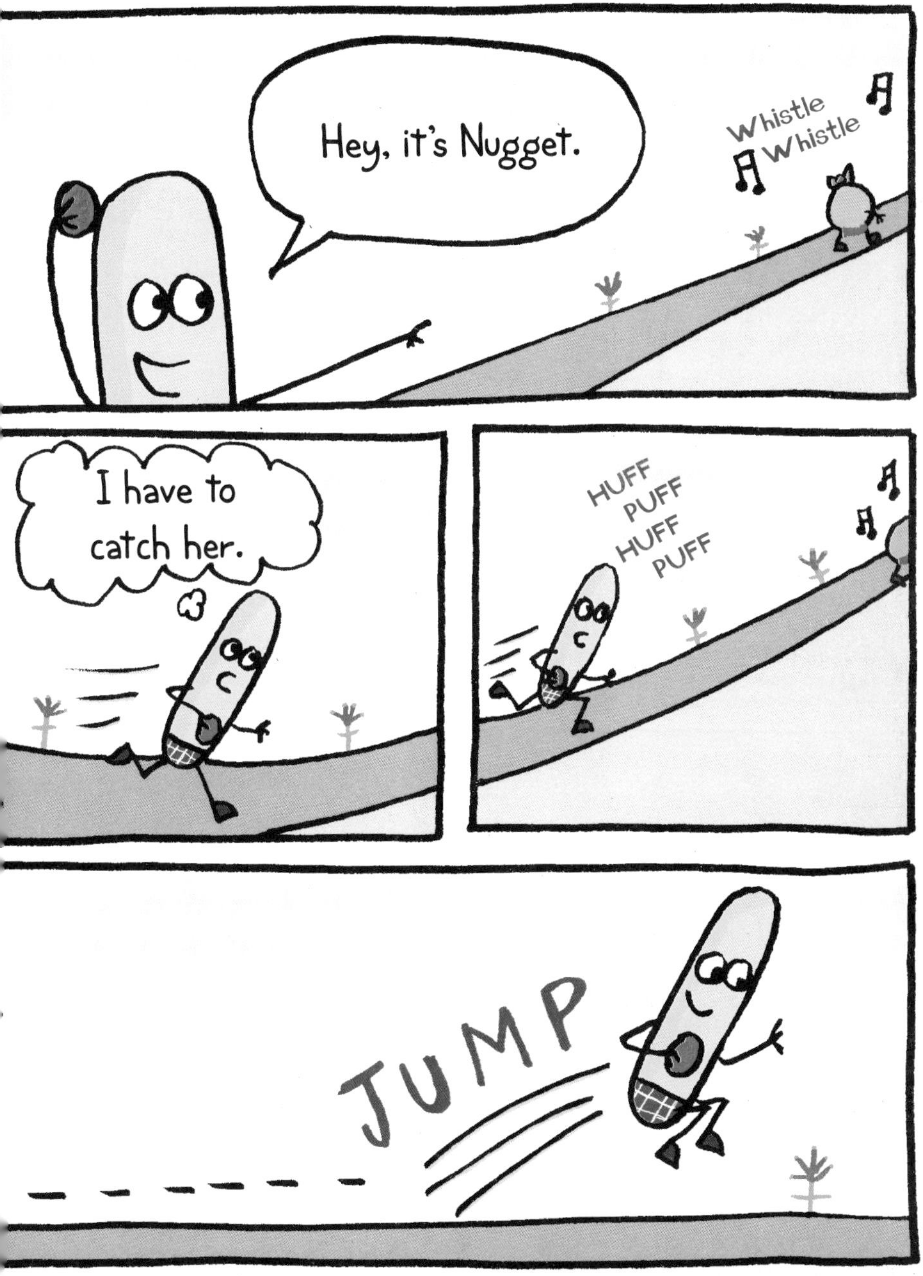
Hey, it's Nugget.
Whistle
Whistle
I have to catch her.
HUFF
PUFF
HUFF
PUFF
JUMP

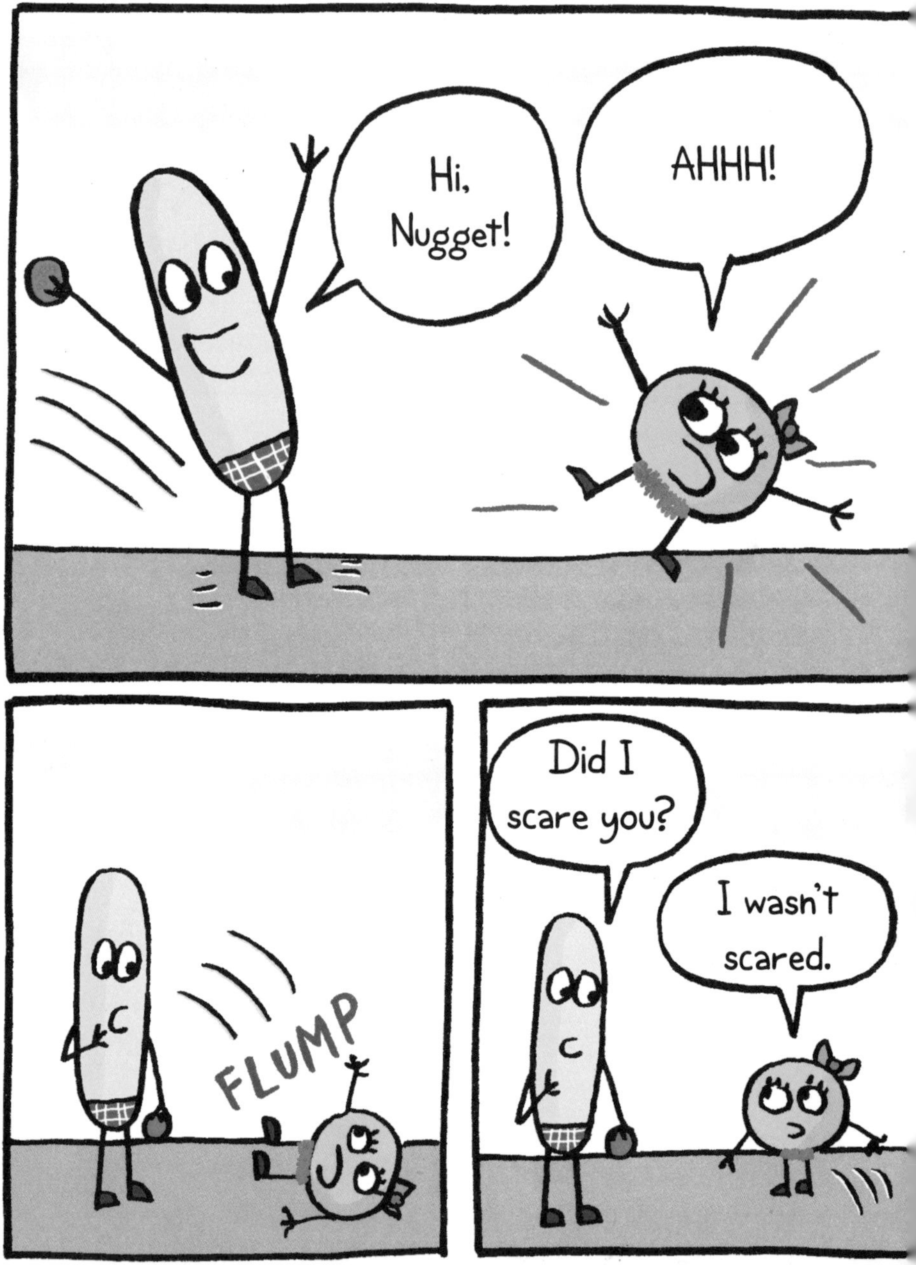
Hi, Nugget!
AHHH!
FLUMP
Did I scare you?
I wasn't scared.

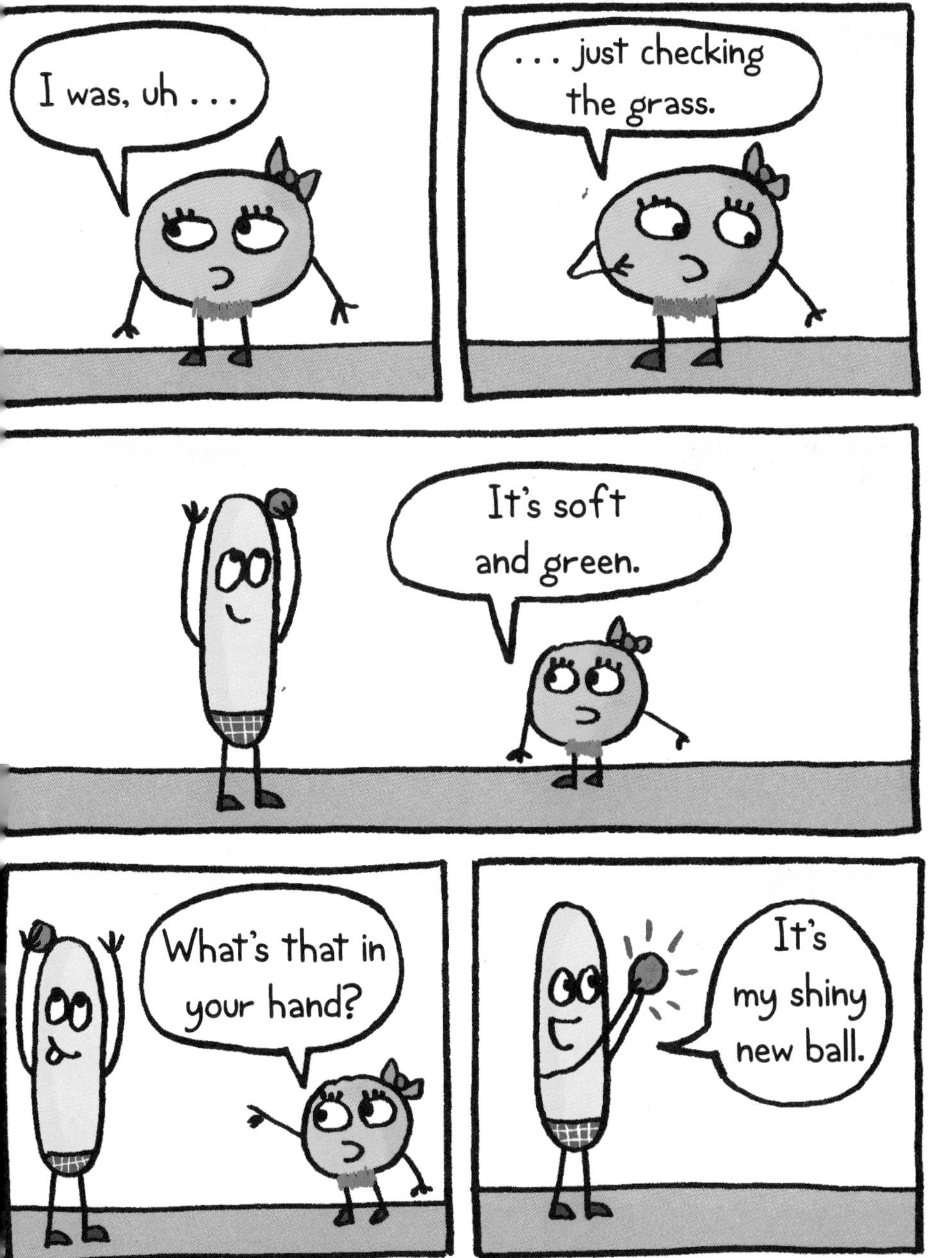
I was, uh . . .
. . . just checking the grass.
It's soft and green.
What's that in your hand?
It's my shiny new ball.

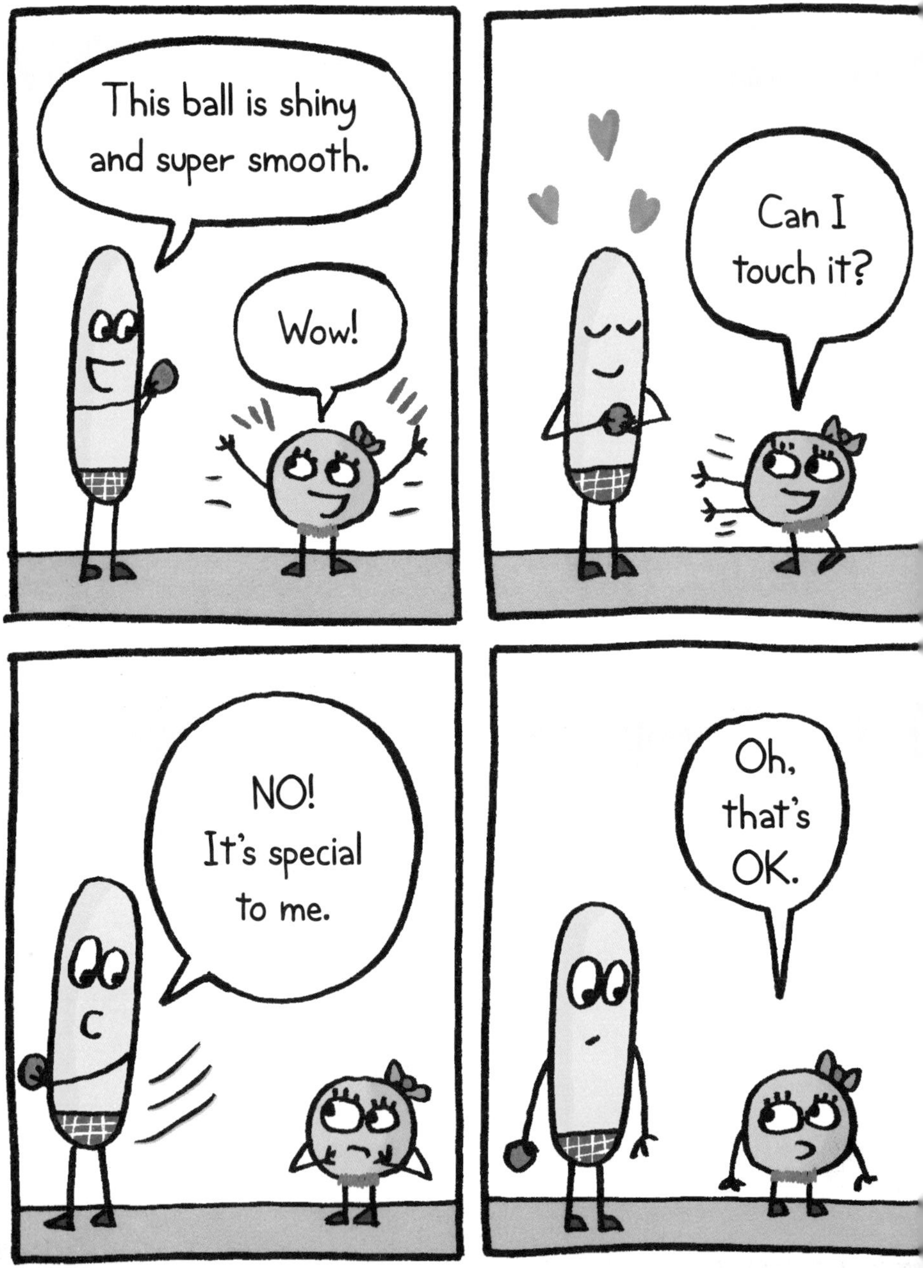
This ball is shiny and super smooth.
Wow!
Can I touch it?
NO! It's special to me.
Oh, that's OK.

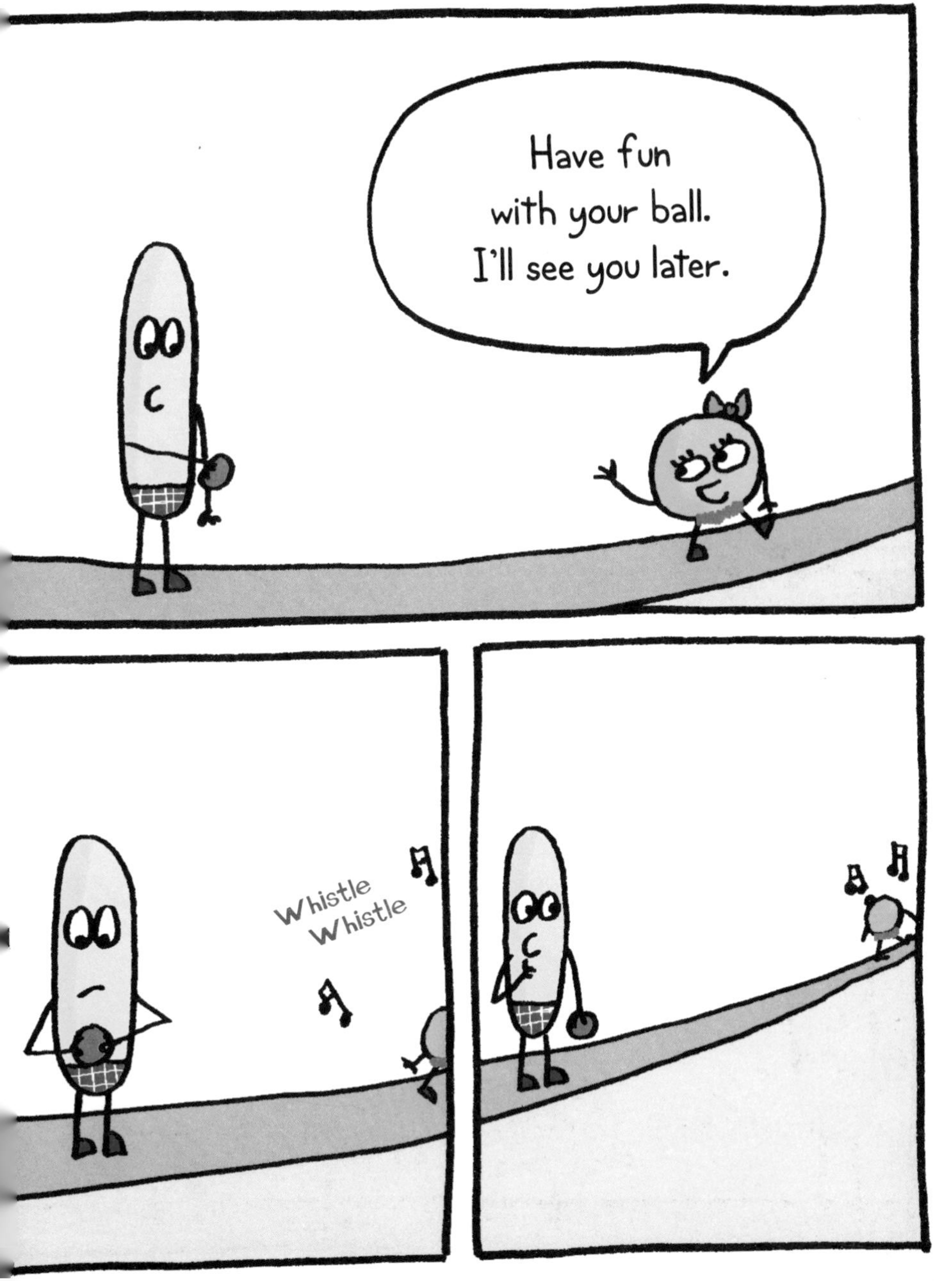
Have fun with your ball. I'll see you later.
Whistle Whistle

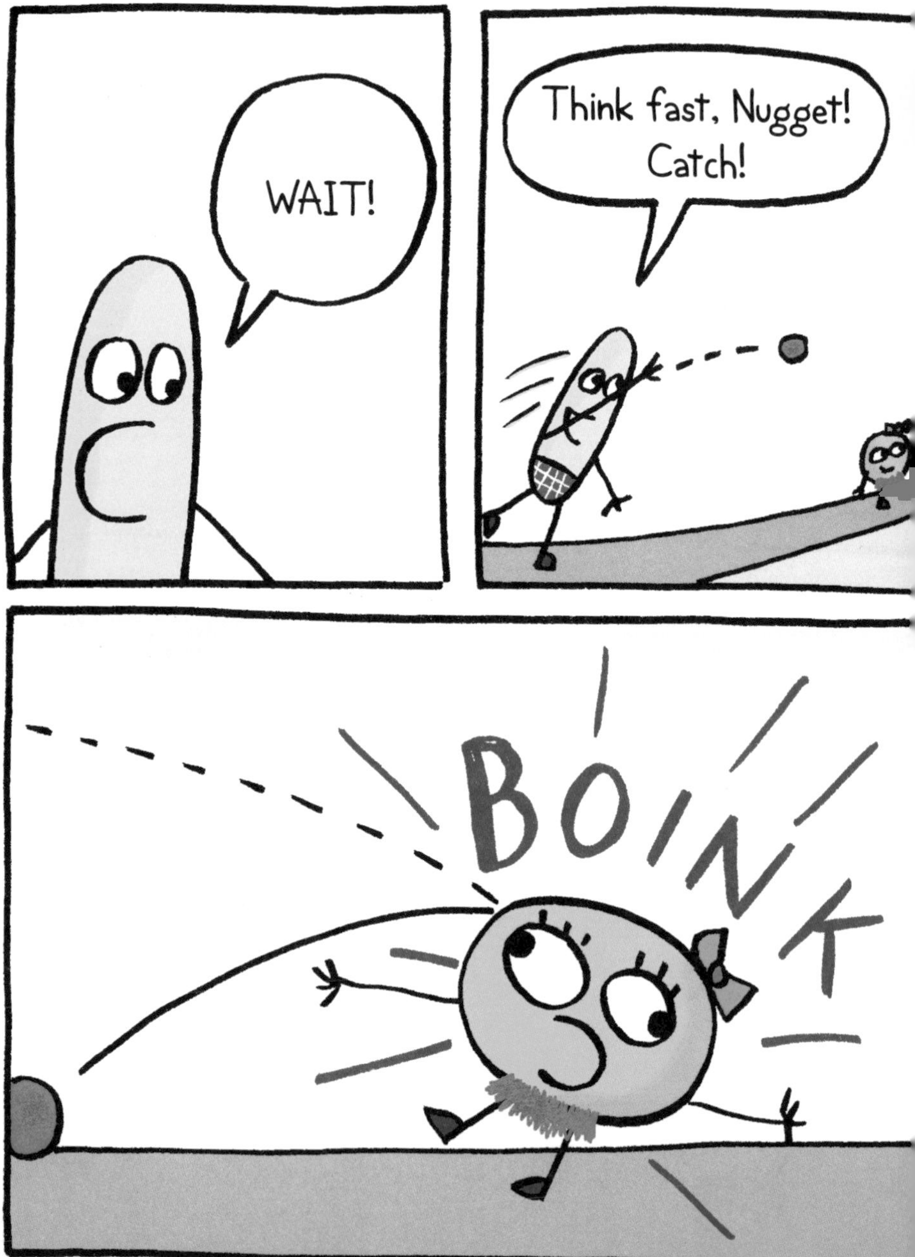
WAIT!
Think fast, Nugget! Catch!
BOINK

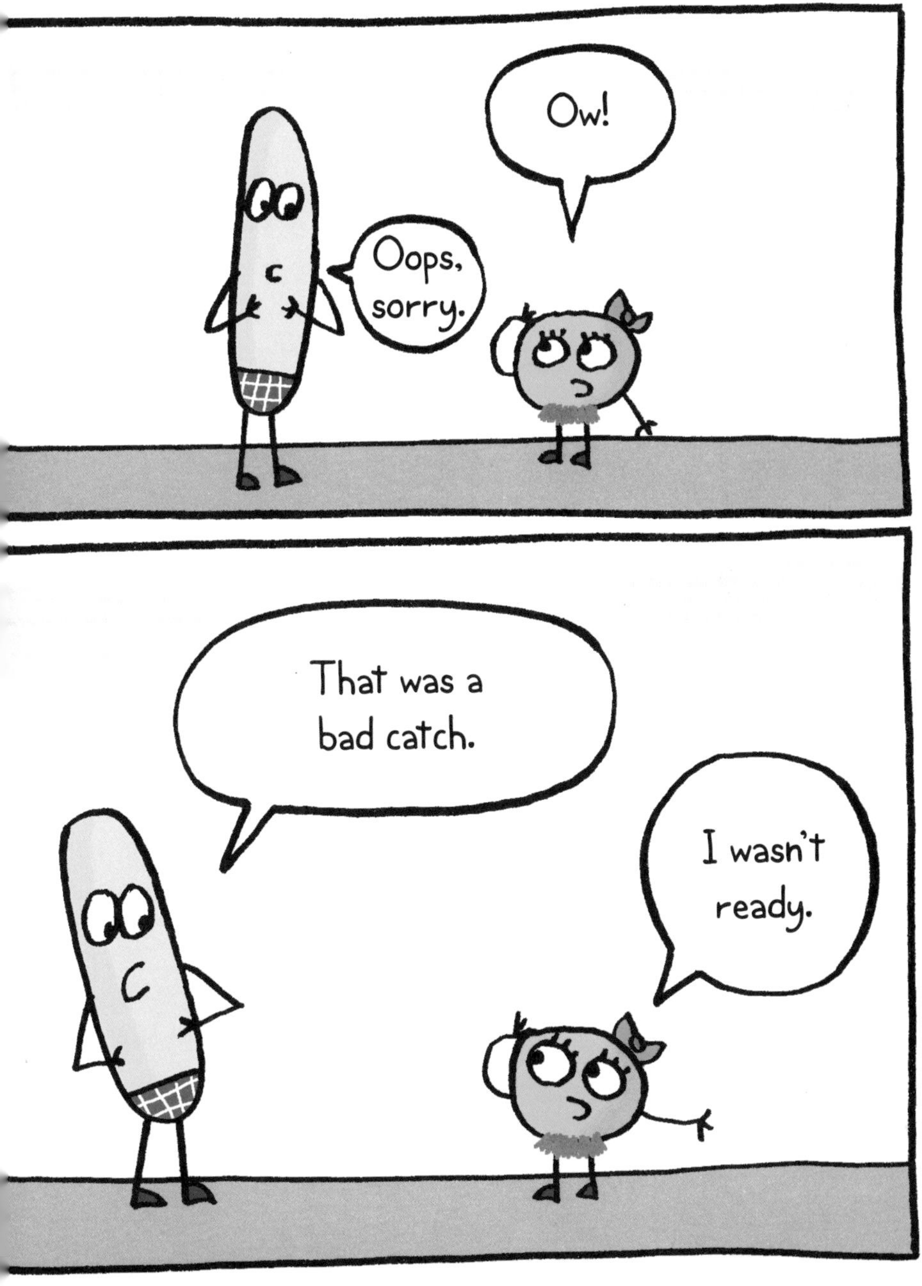
Ow!
Oops, sorry.
That was a bad catch.
I wasn't ready.

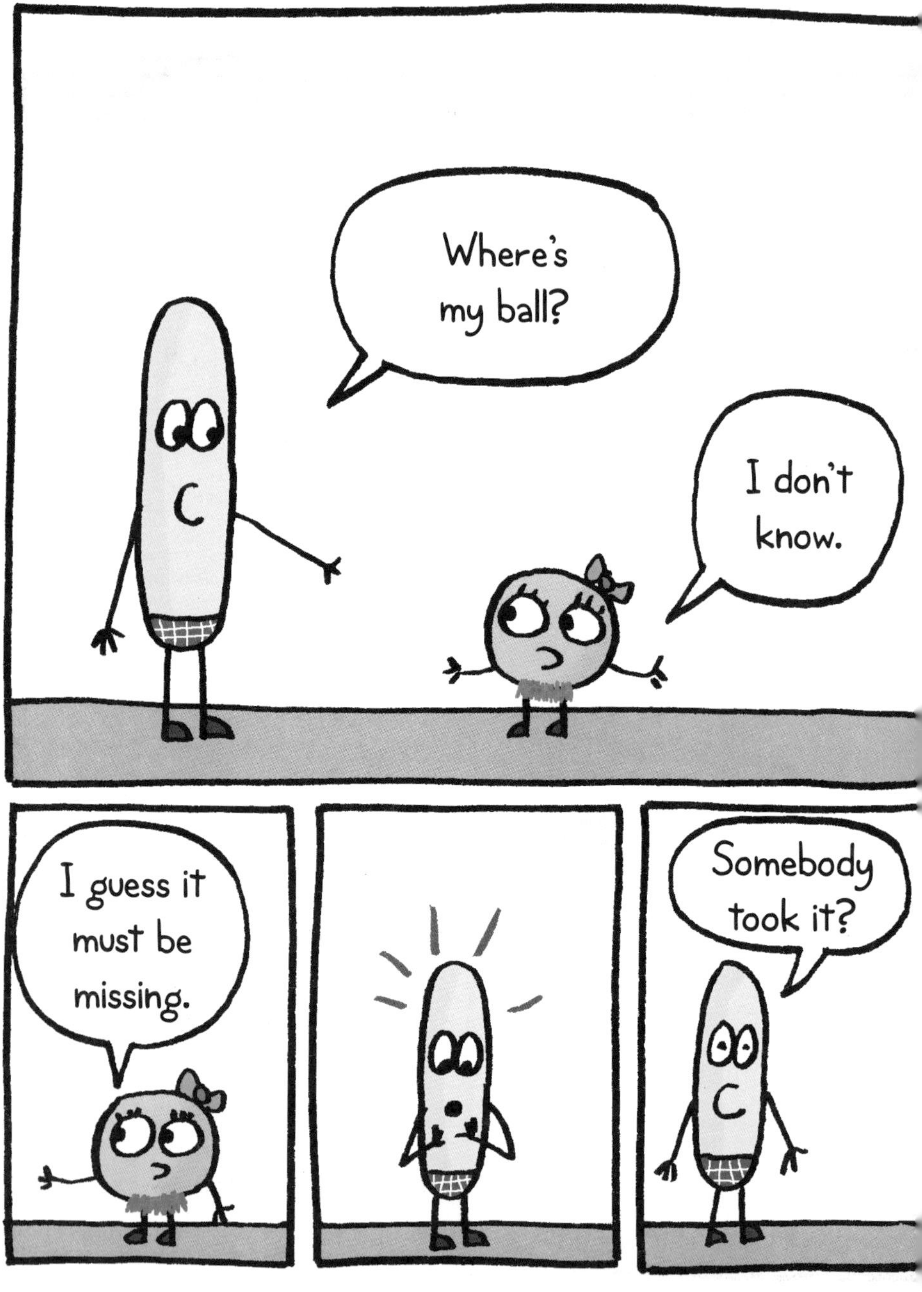
Where's my ball?
I don't know.
I guess it must be missing.
Somebody took it?

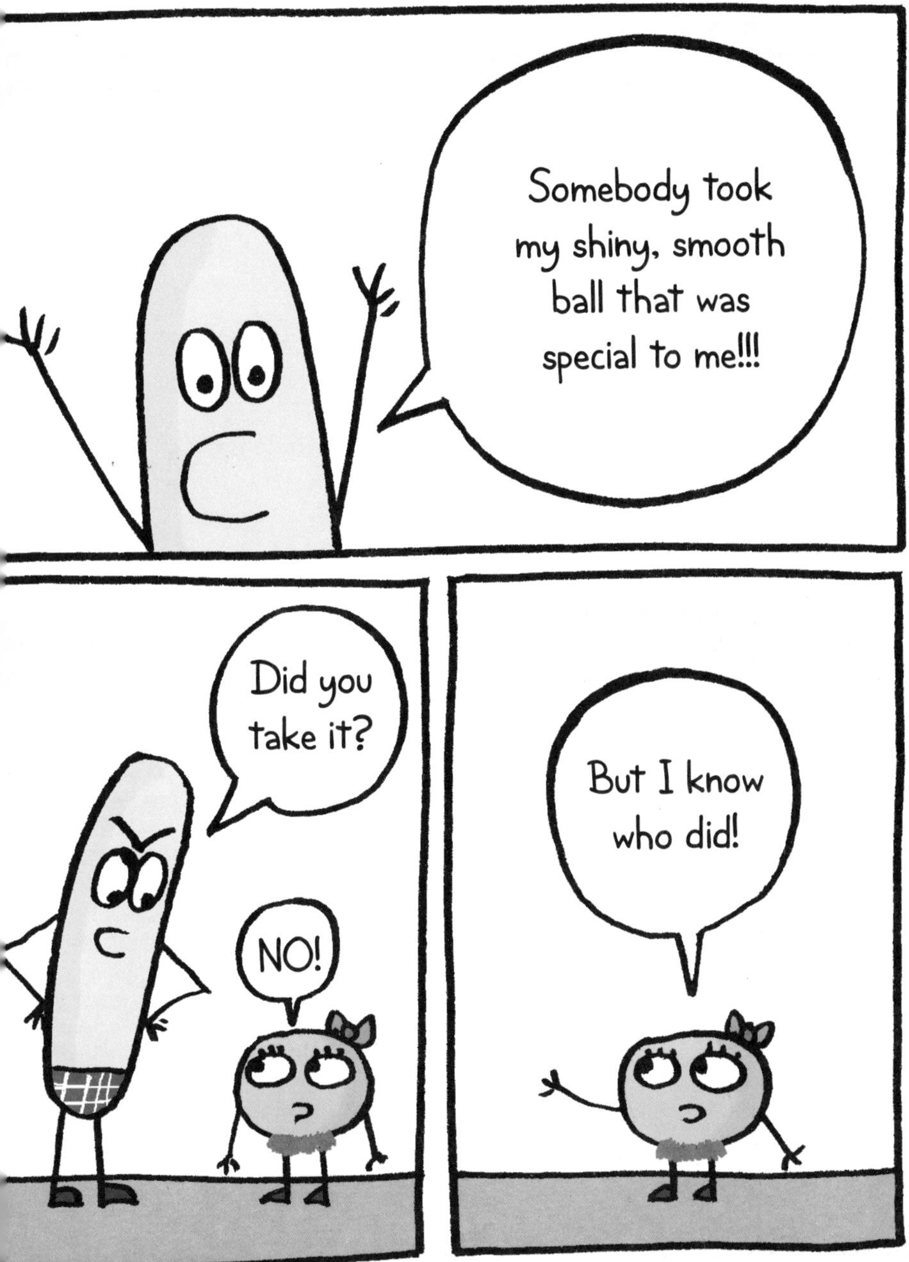
Somebody took my shiny, smooth ball that was special to me!!!
Did you take it?
NO!
But I know who did!

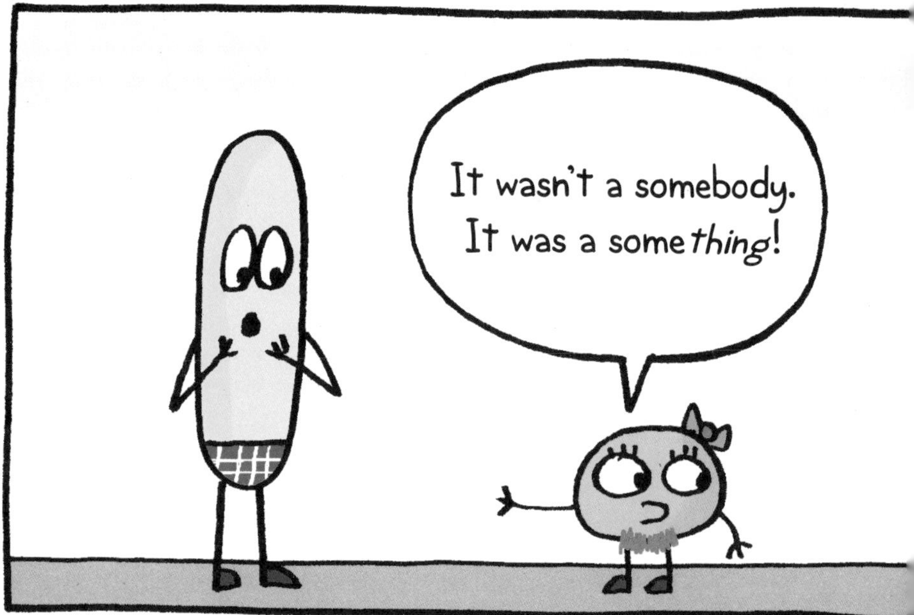
It wasn't a somebody. It was a something!

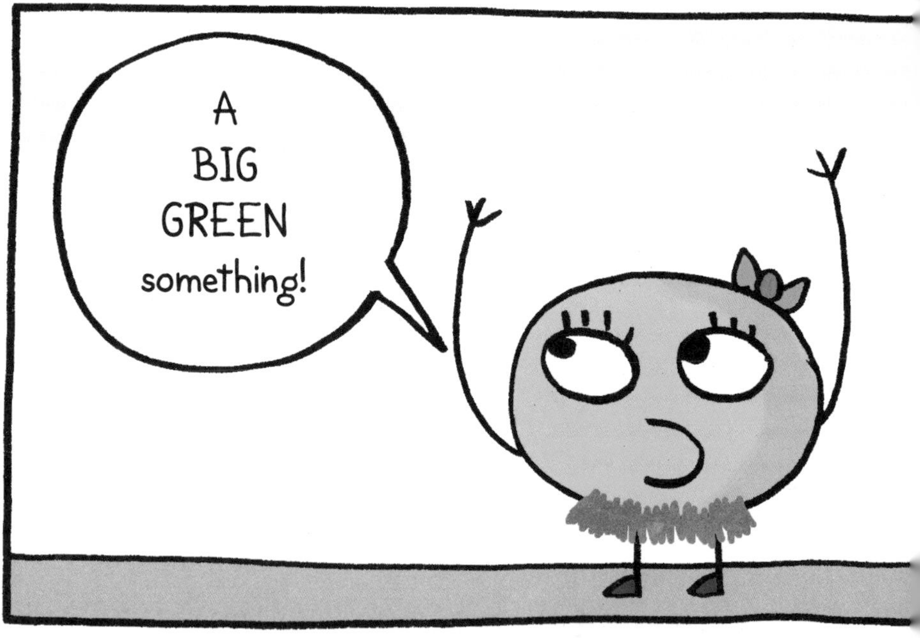
A BIG GREEN something!

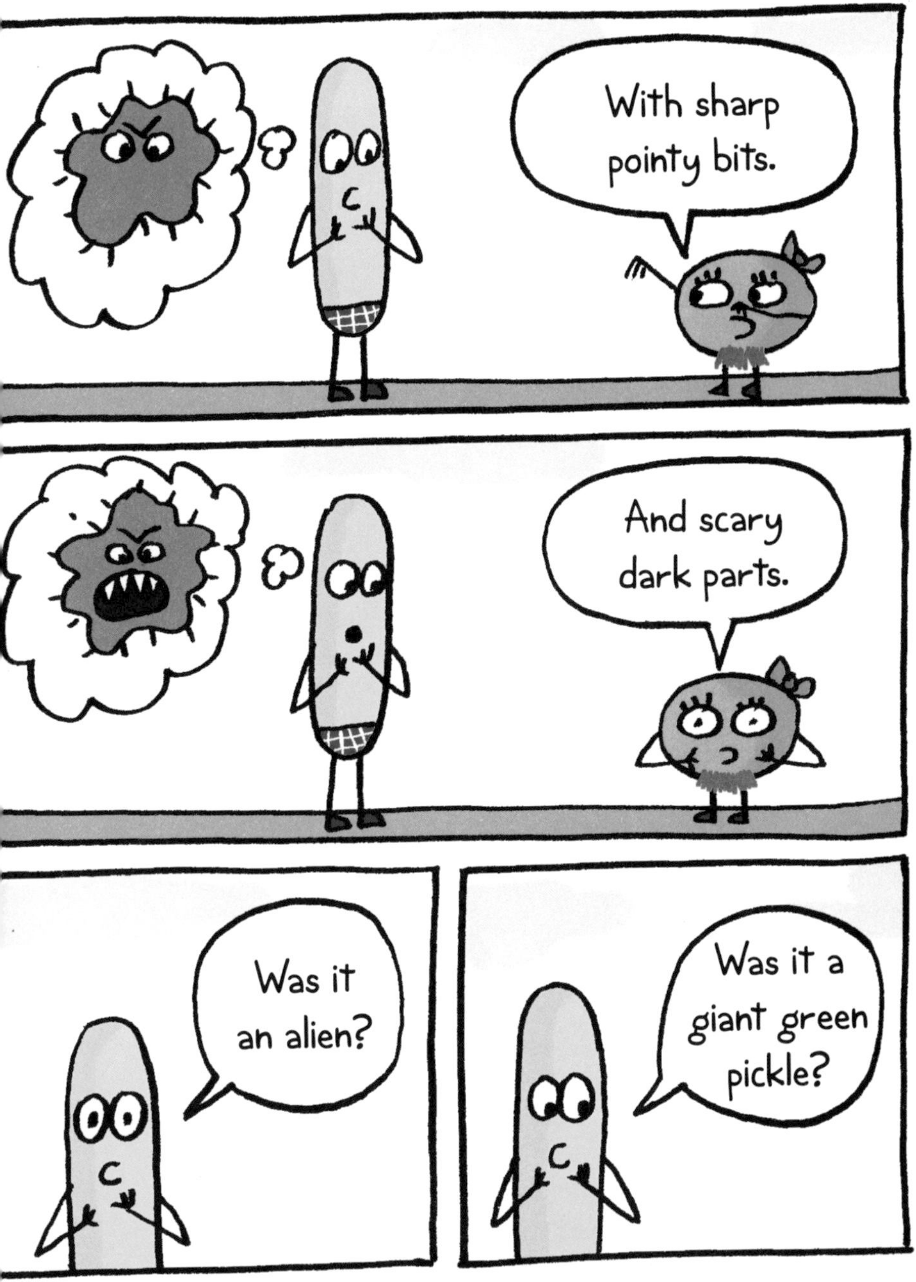
With sharp pointy bits.
And scary dark parts.
Was it an alien?
Was it a giant green pickle?

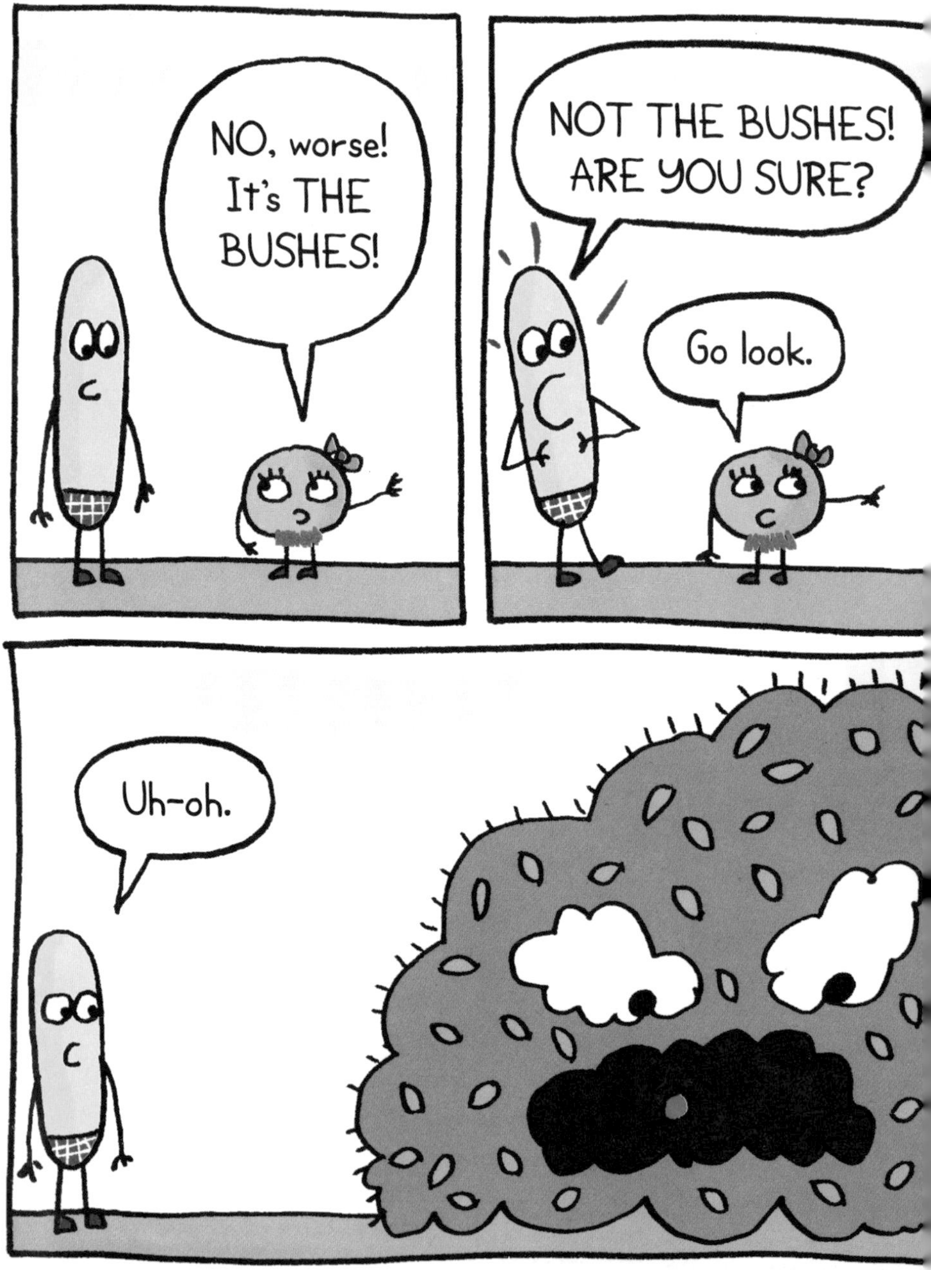
NO, worse! It's THE BUSHES!
NOT THE BUSHES! ARE YOU SURE?
Go look.
Uh-oh.

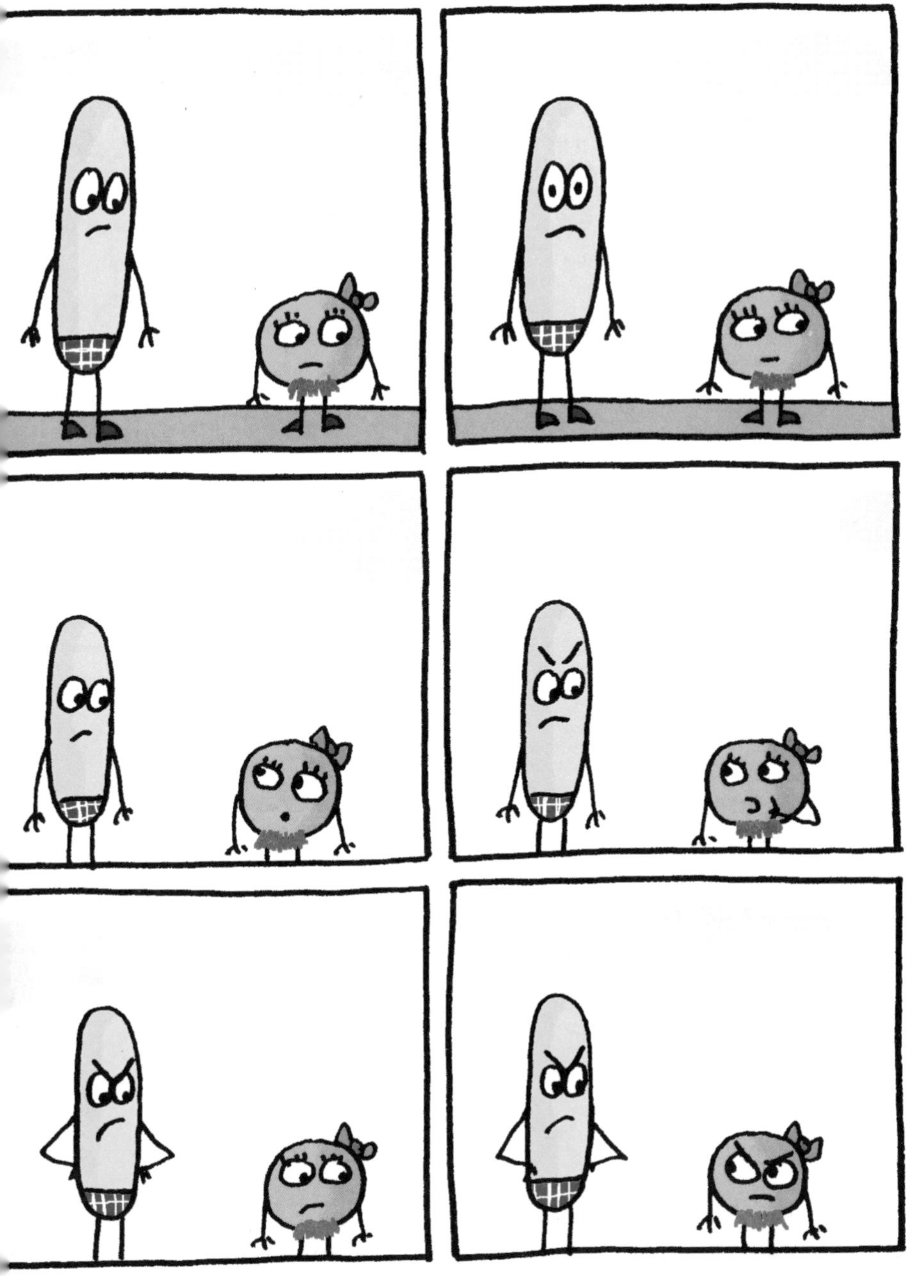

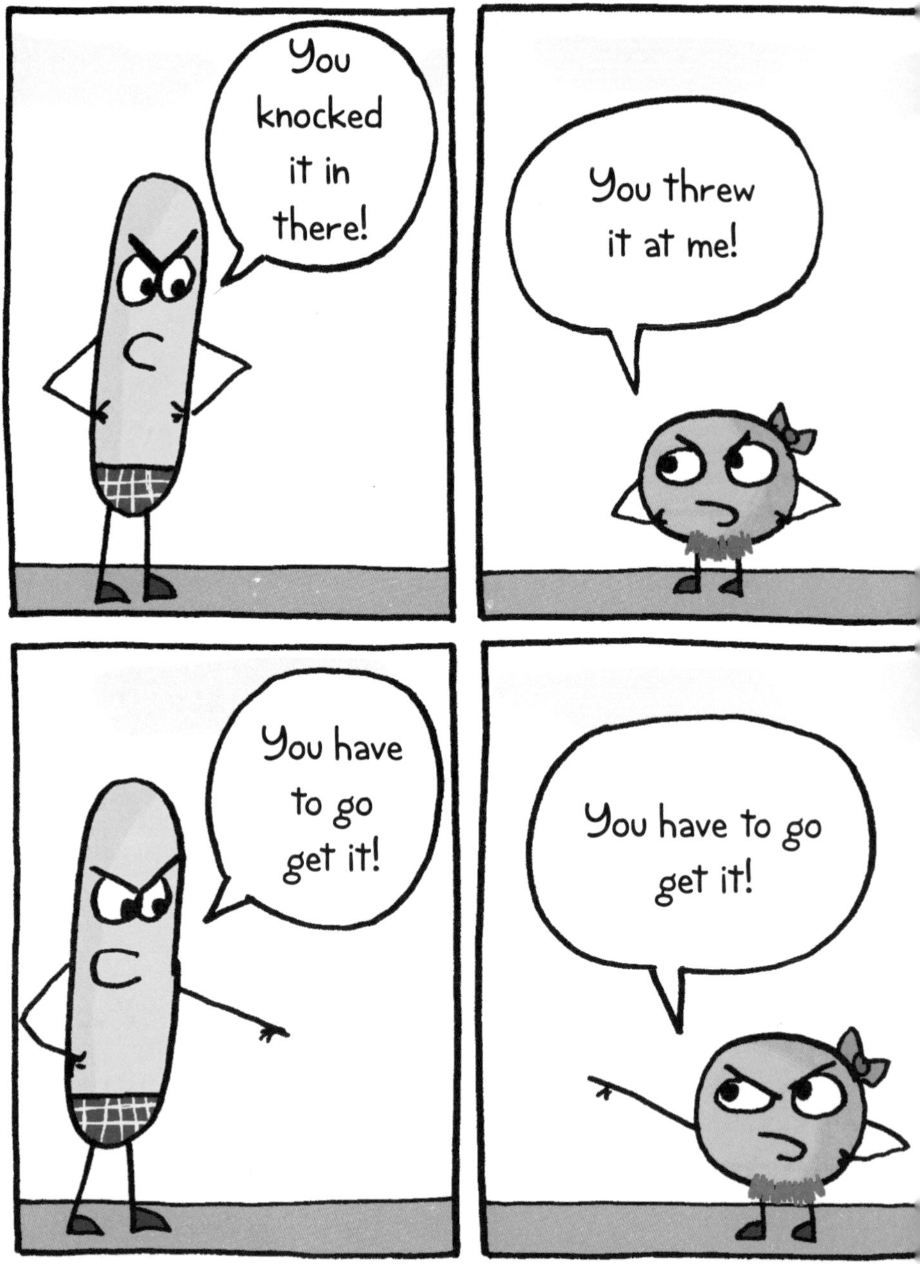

You knocked it in there!
You threw it at me!
You have to go get it!
You have to go get it!

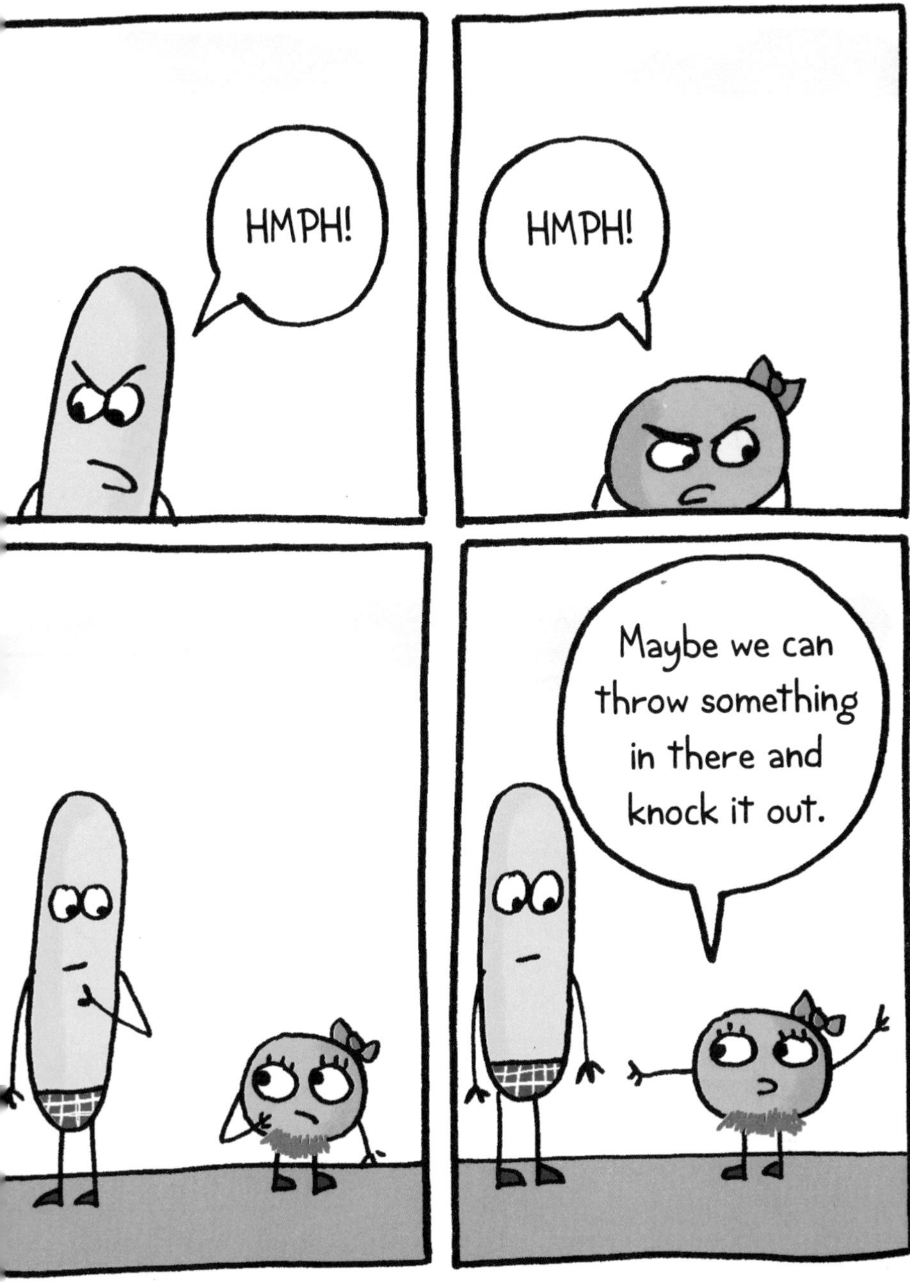
HMPH!
HMPH!
Maybe we can throw something in there and knock it out.

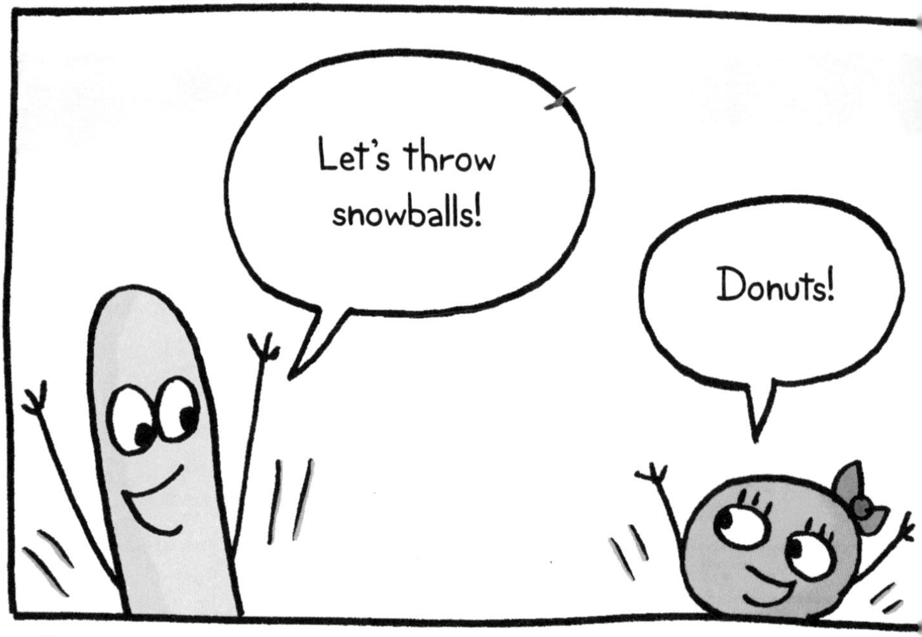
Let's throw snowballs!
Donuts!

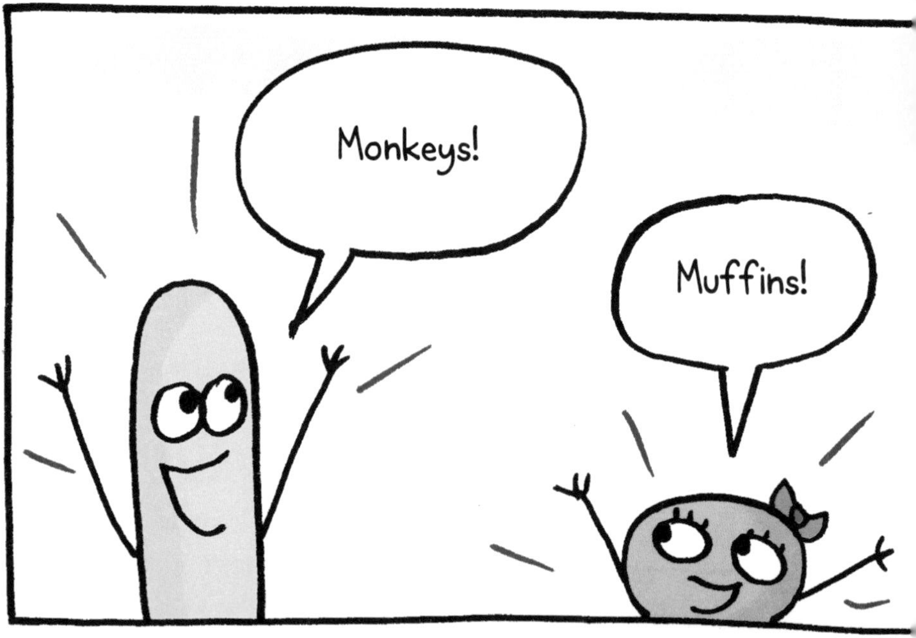
Monkeys!
Muffins!

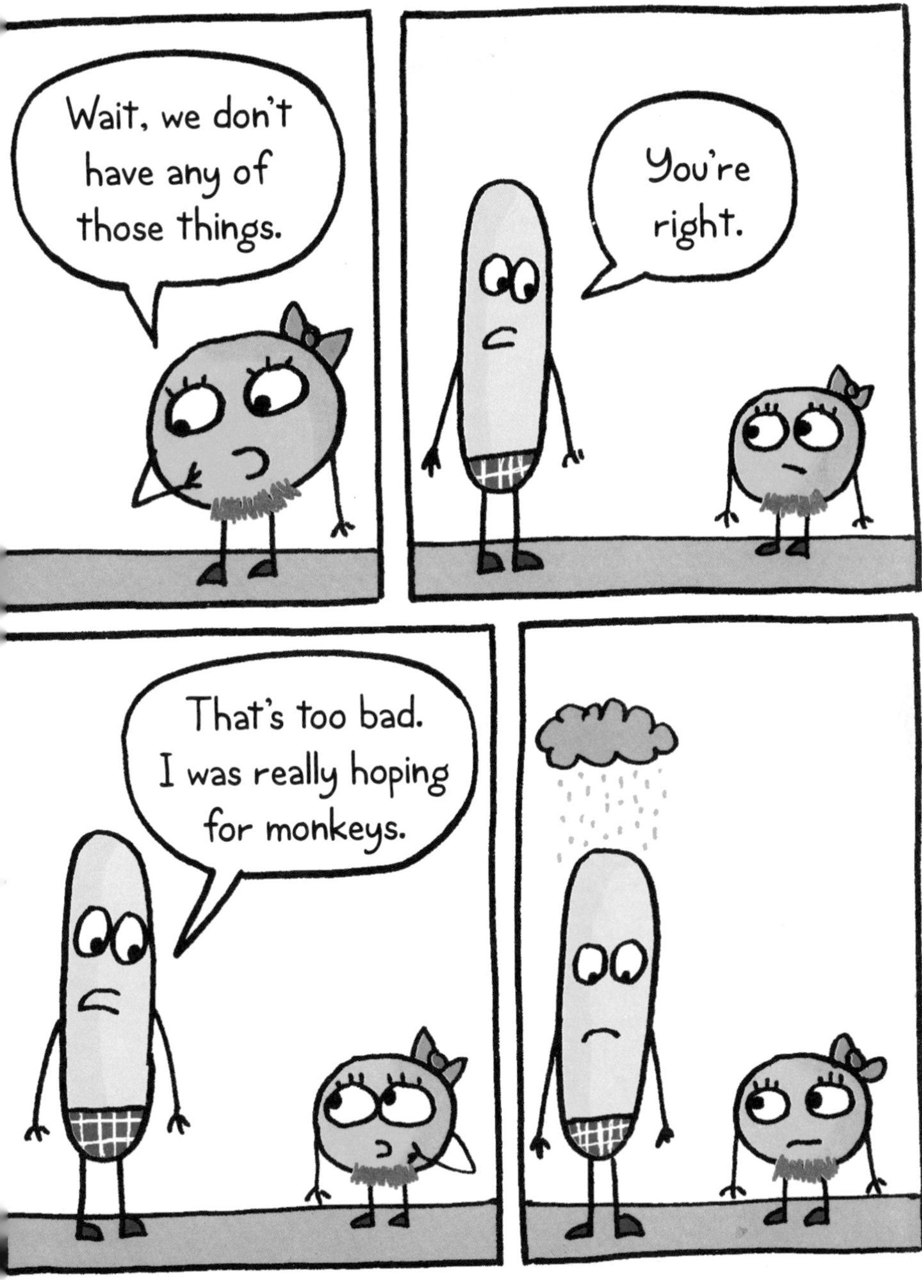
Wait, we don't have any of those things.
You're right.
That's too bad. I was really hoping for monkeys.

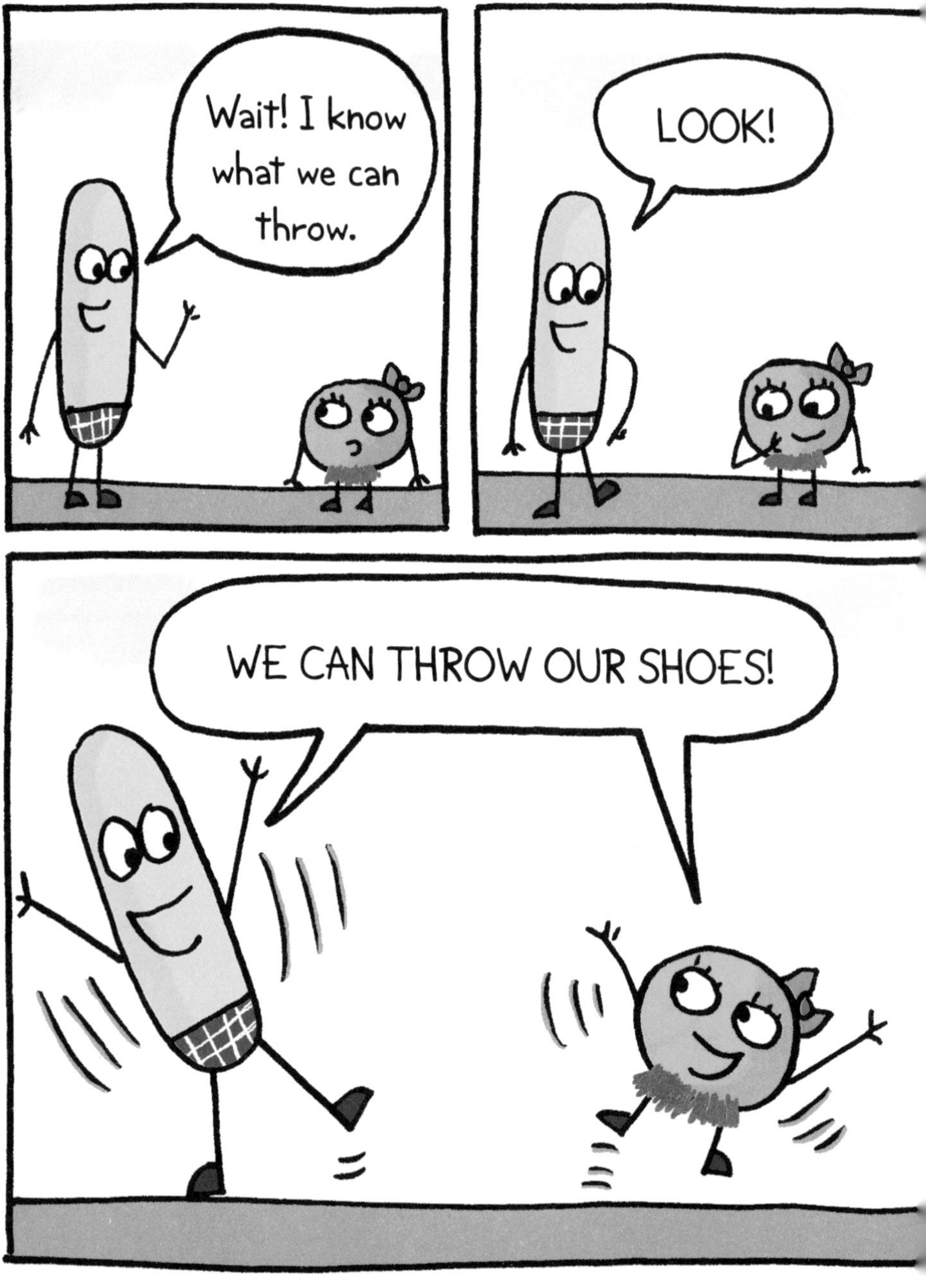
Wait! I know what we can throw.
LOOK!
WE CAN THROW OUR SHOES!

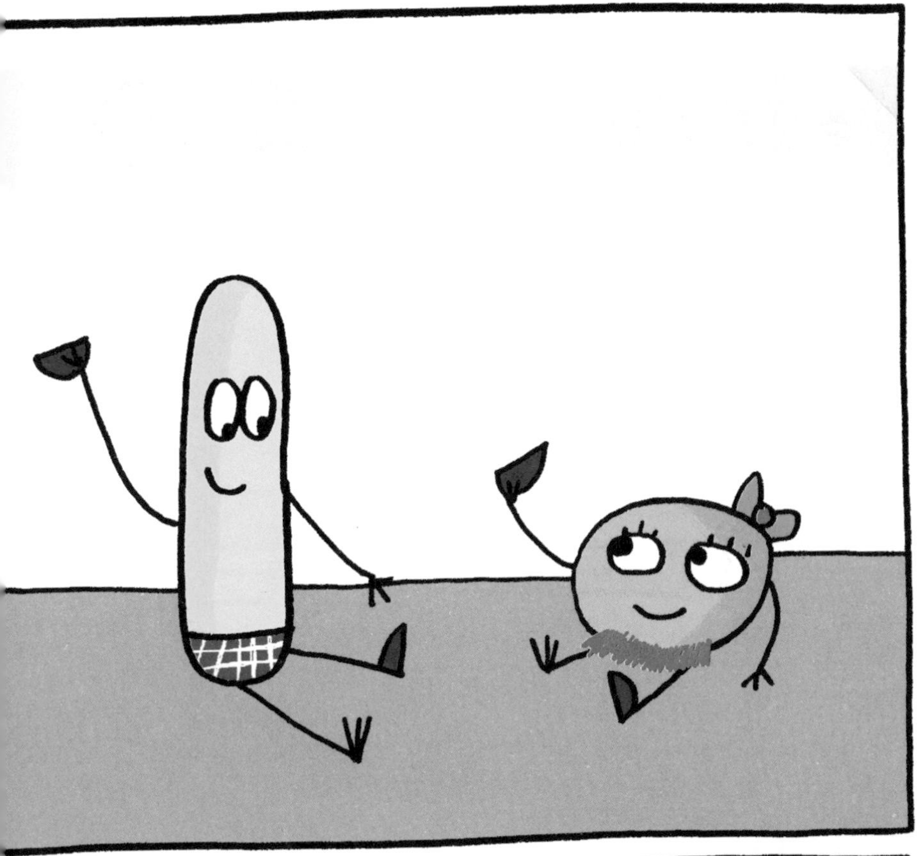

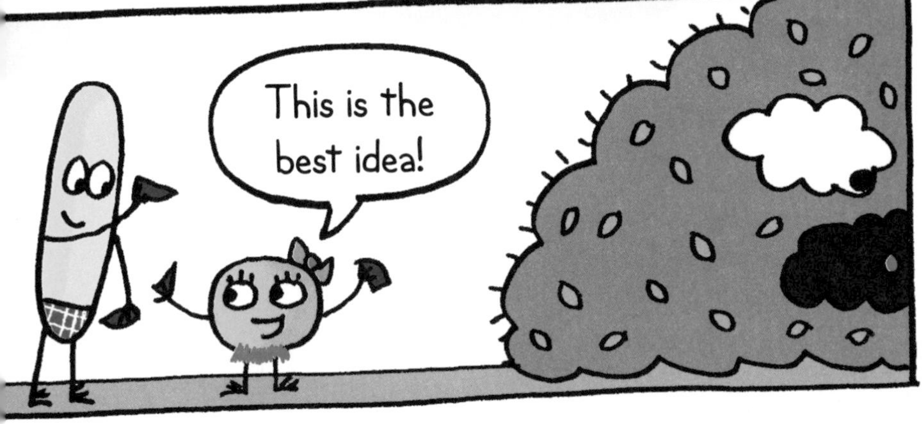
This is the best idea!

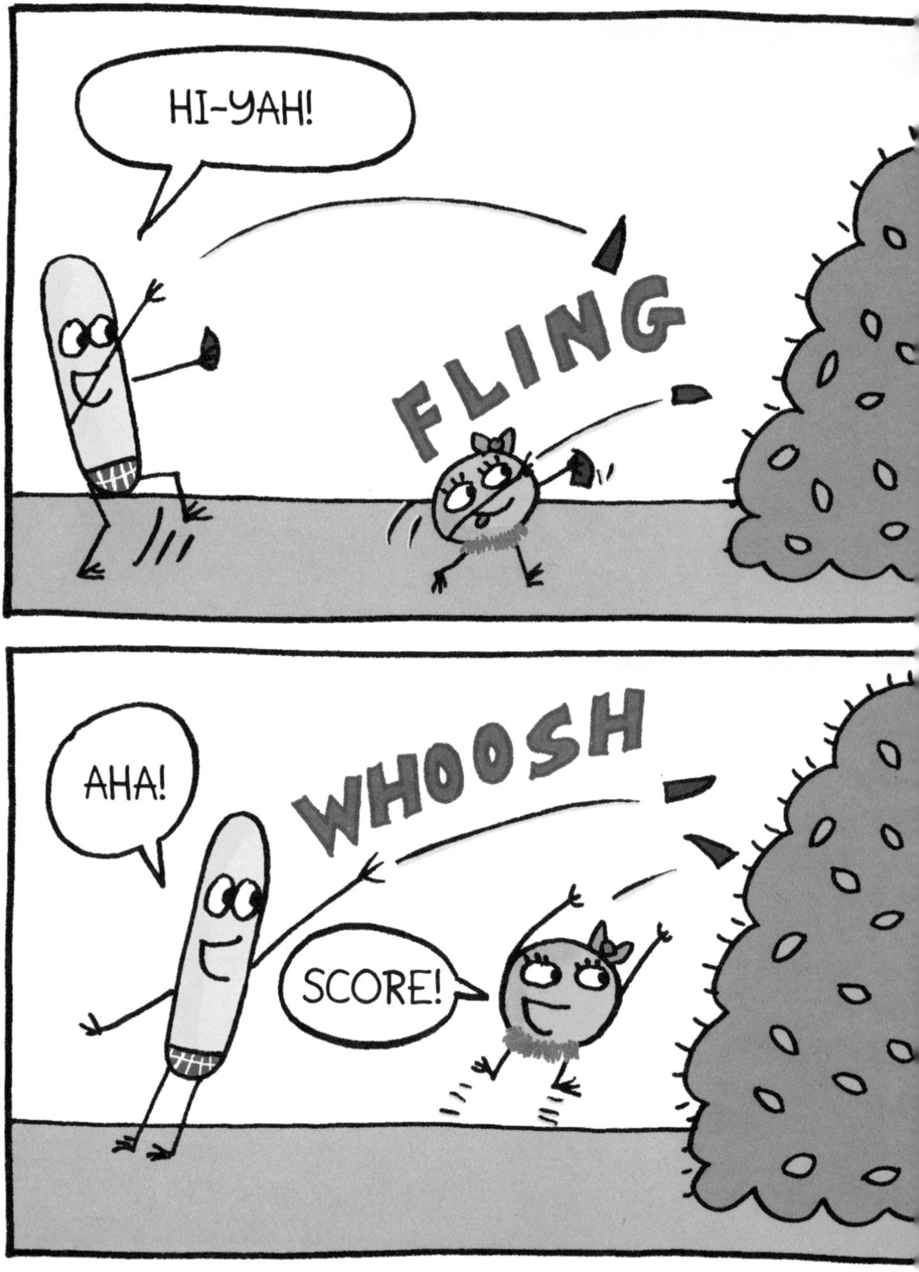
HI-YAH!
FLING
AHA!
WHOOSH
SCORE!

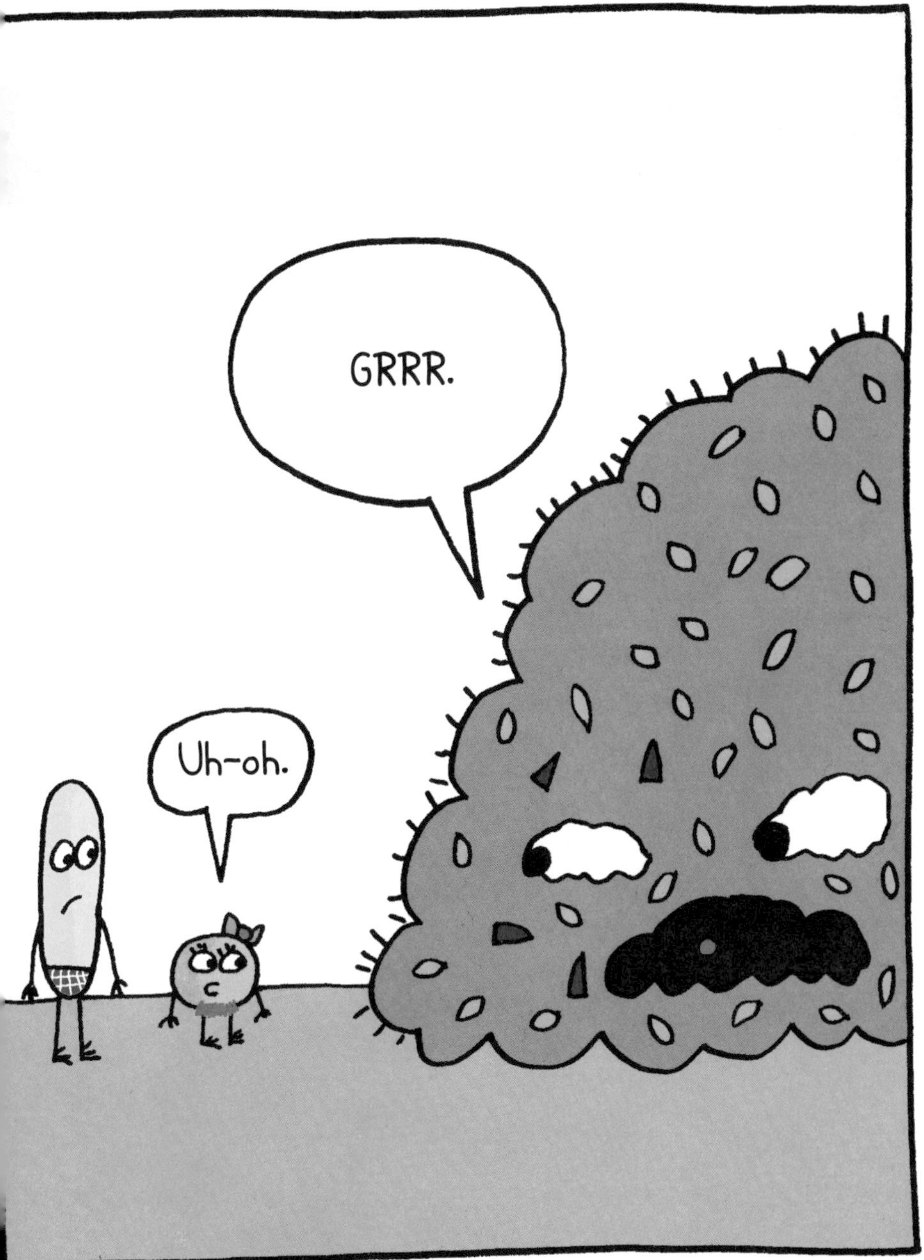
GRRR.
Uh-oh.

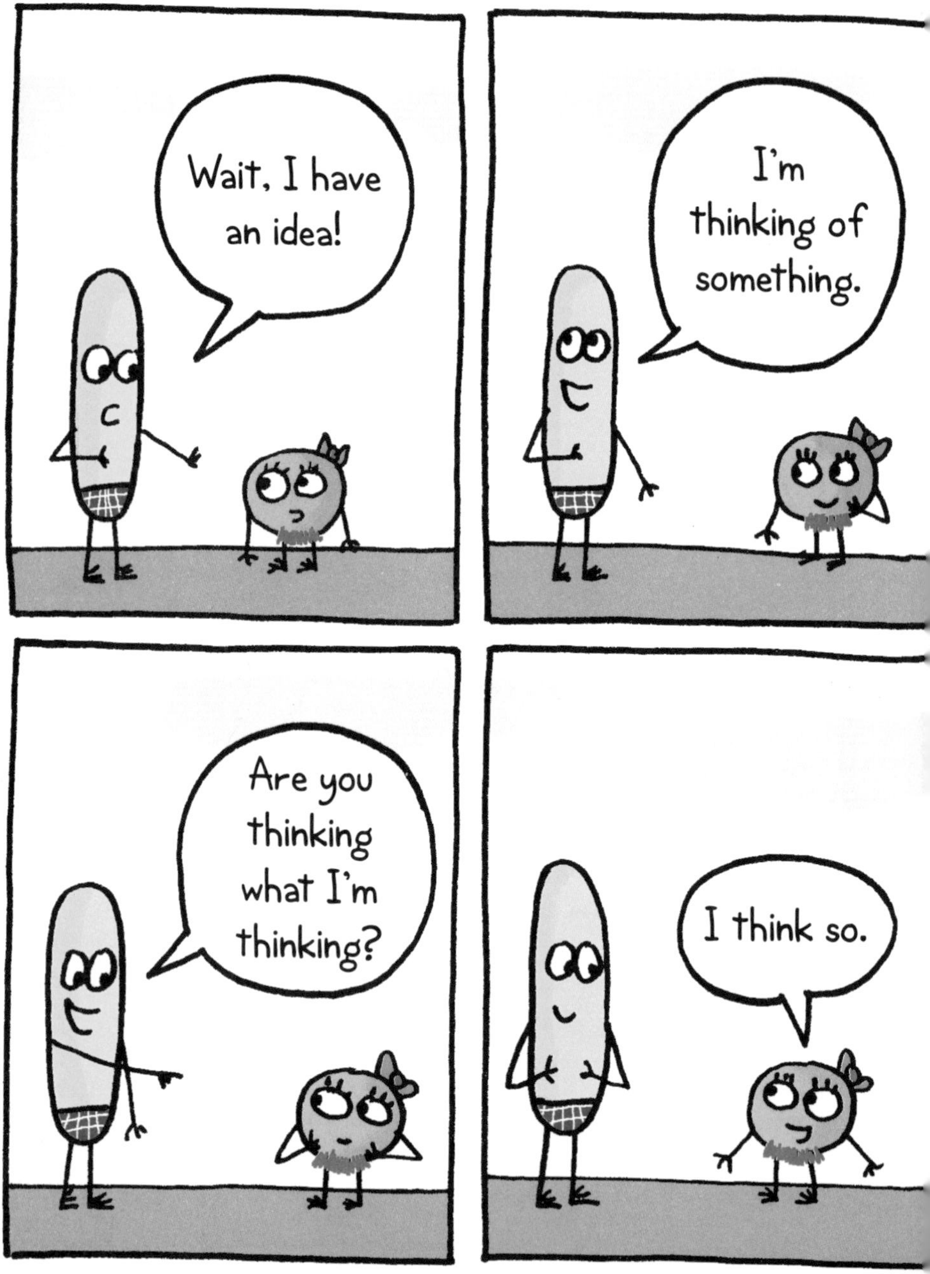
Wait, I have an idea!
I'm thinking of something.
Are you thinking what I'm thinking?
I think so.

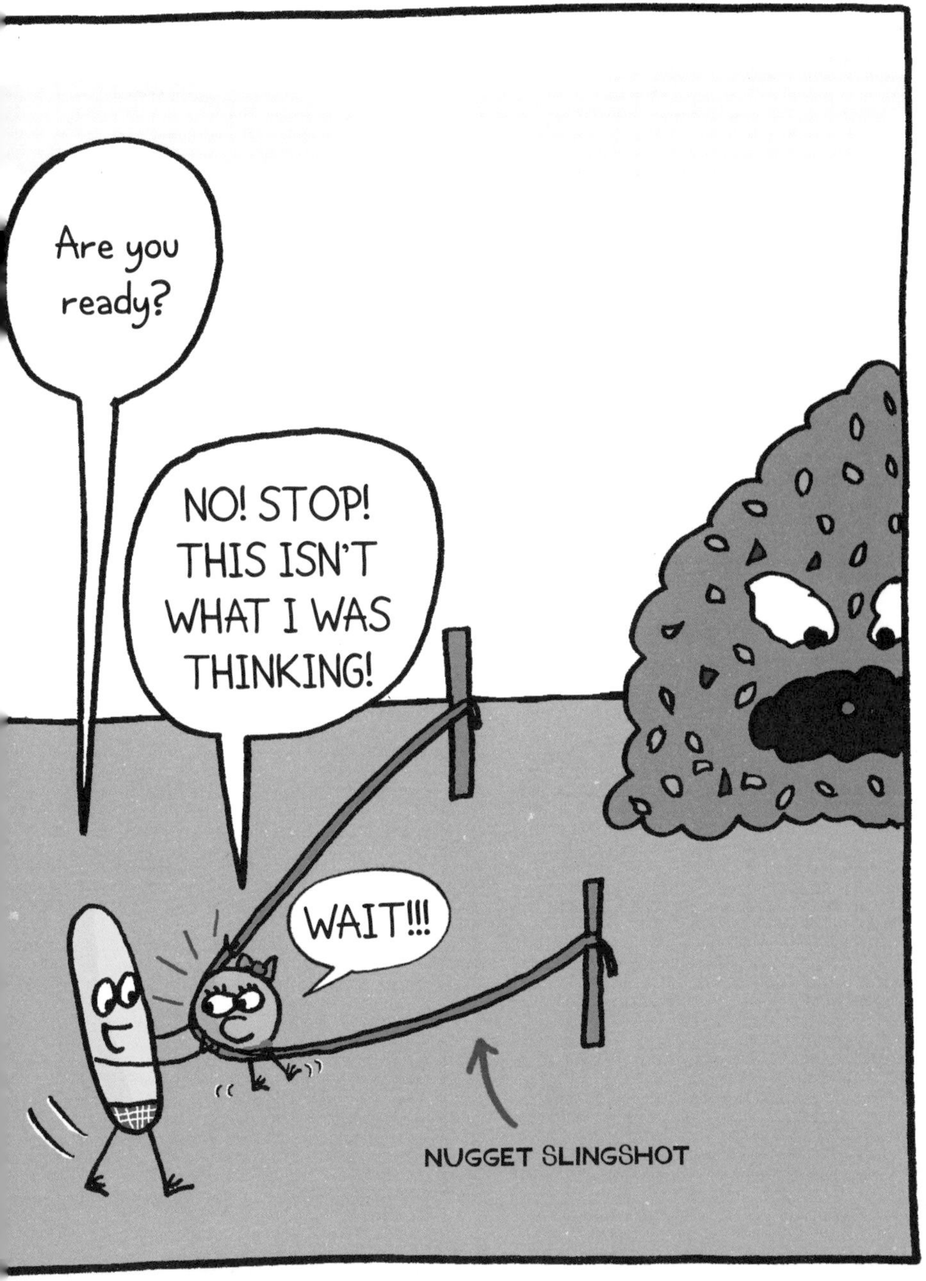

Are you ready?
NO! STOP! THIS ISN'T WHAT I WAS THINKING!
WAIT!!!
NUGGET SLINGSHOT

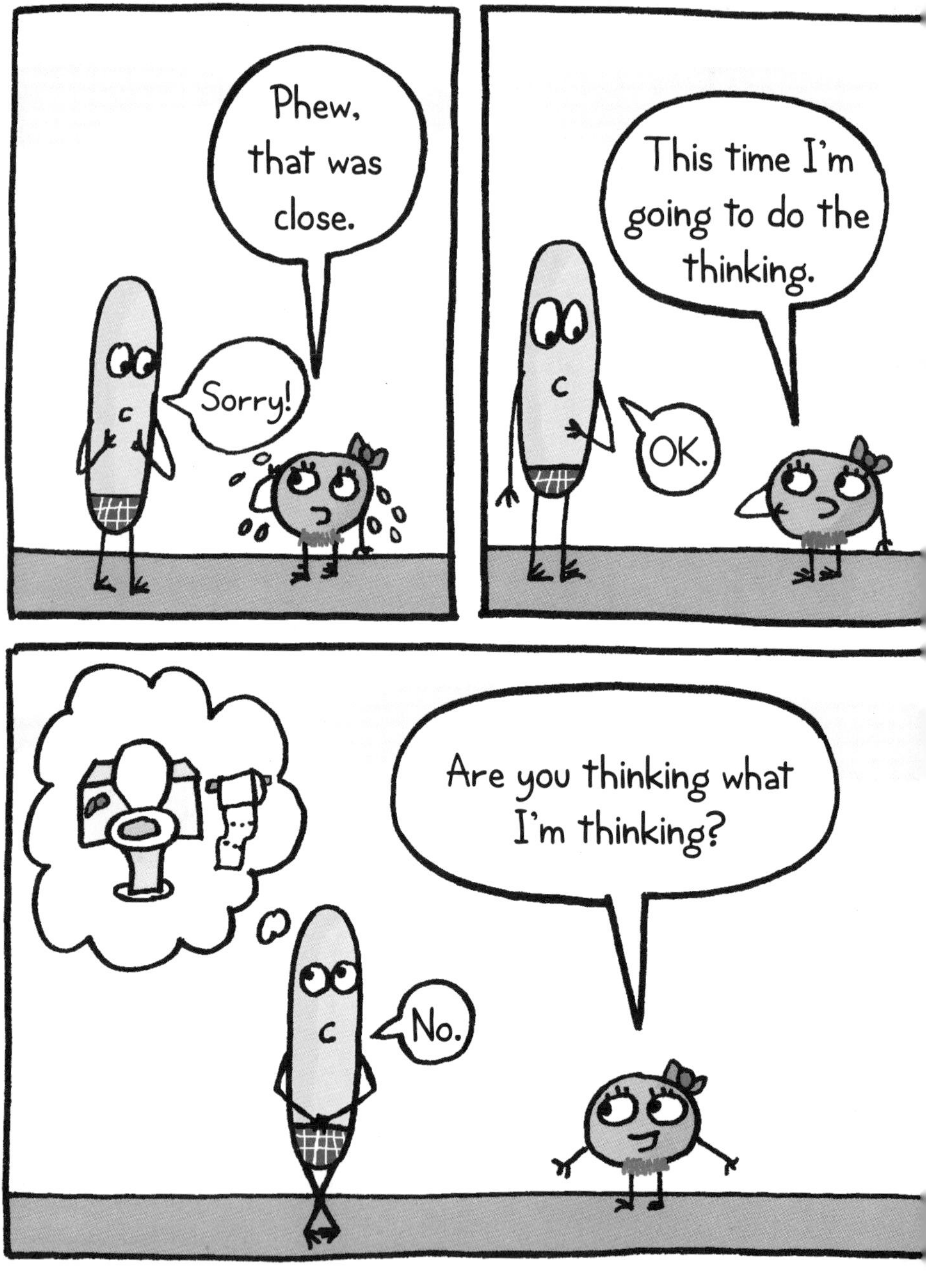
Phew, that was close.
Sorry!
This time I'm going to do the thinking.
OK.
Are you thinking what I'm thinking?
No.

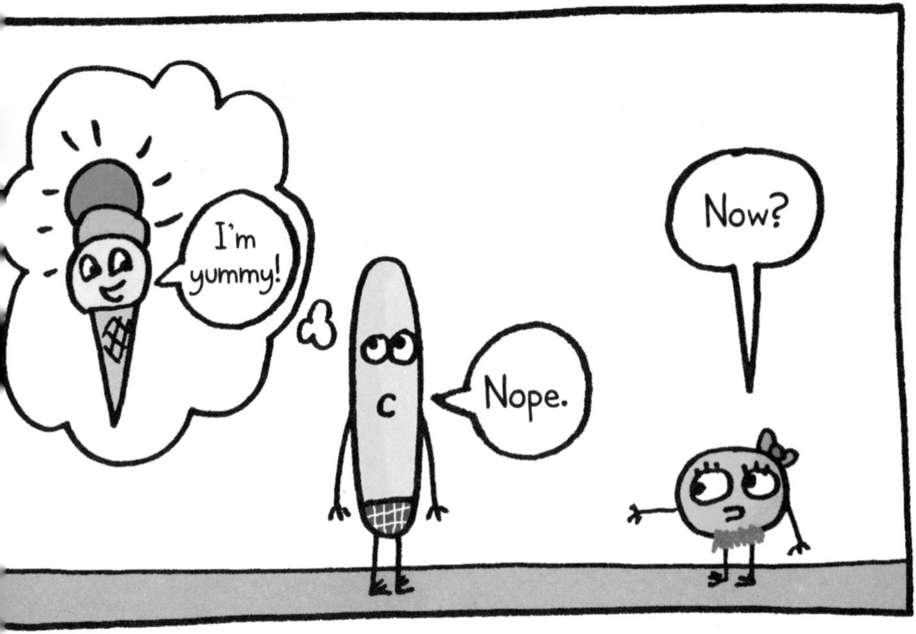
I'm yummy!
Nope.
Now?

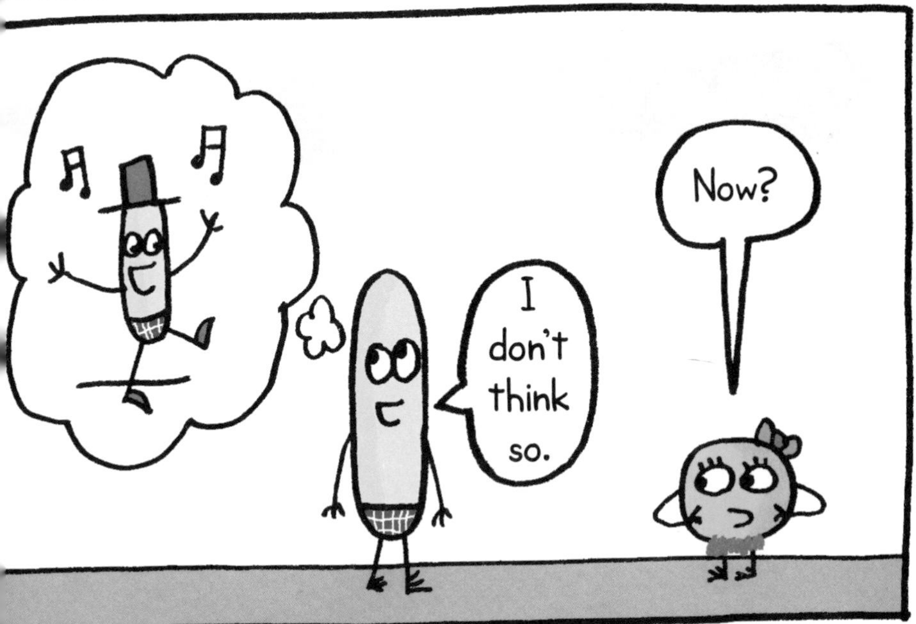
I don't think so.
Now?

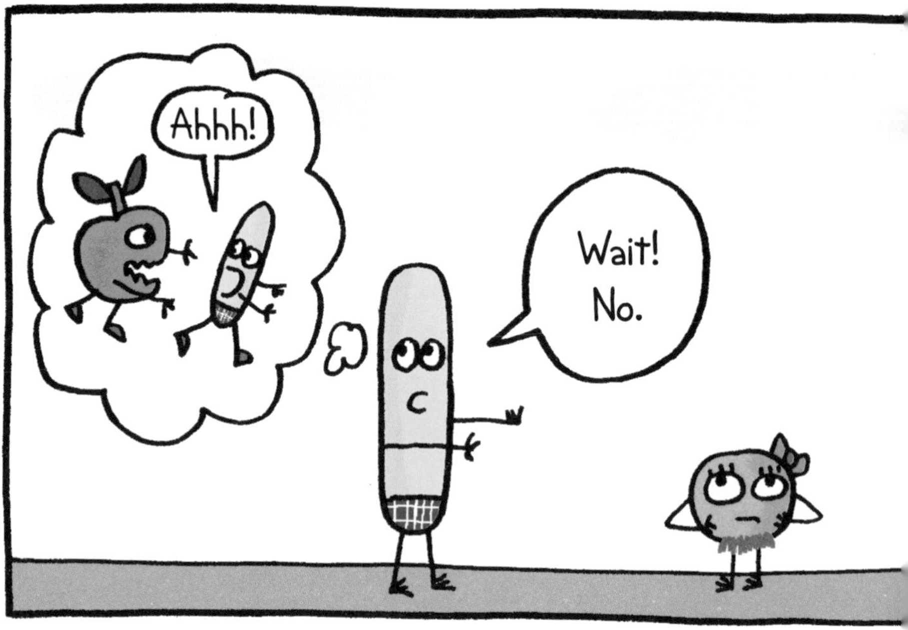
Ahhh!
Wait! No.

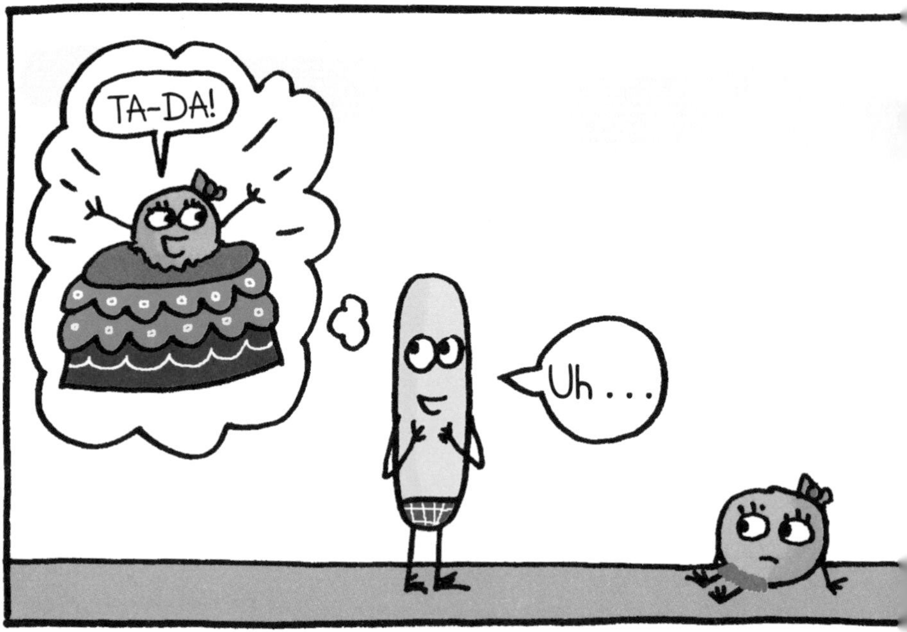
TA-DA!
Uh . . .

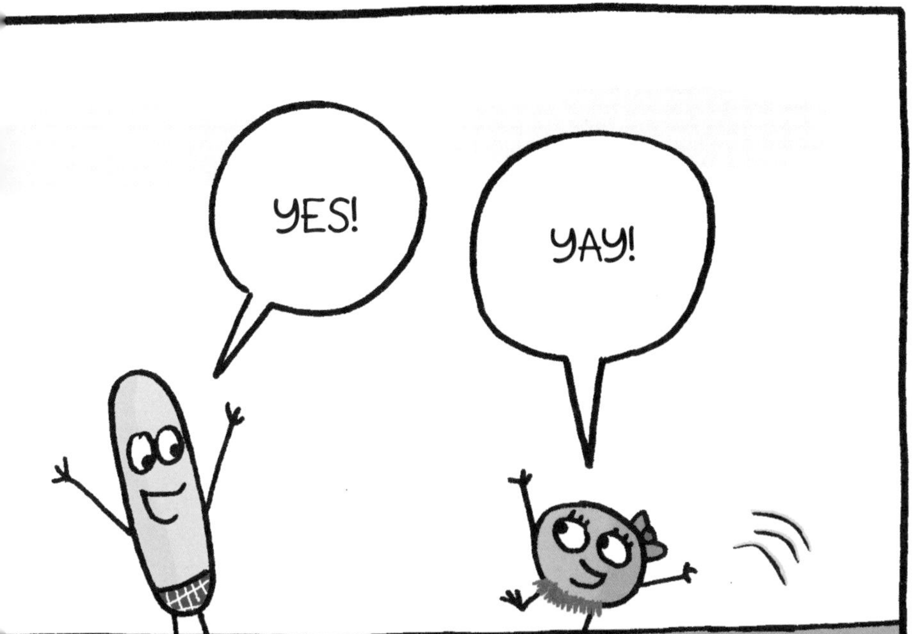
YES!
YAY!

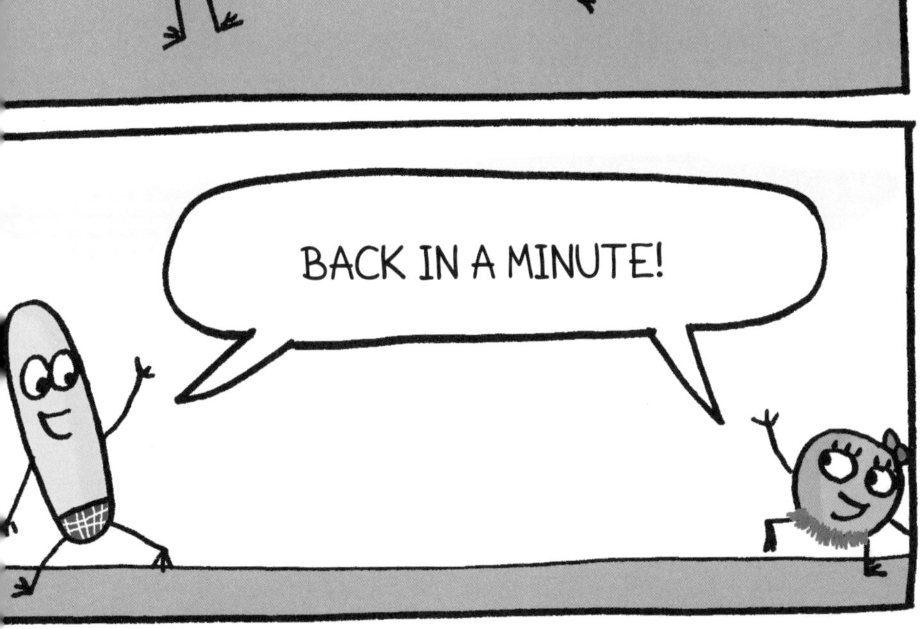
BACK IN A MINUTE!

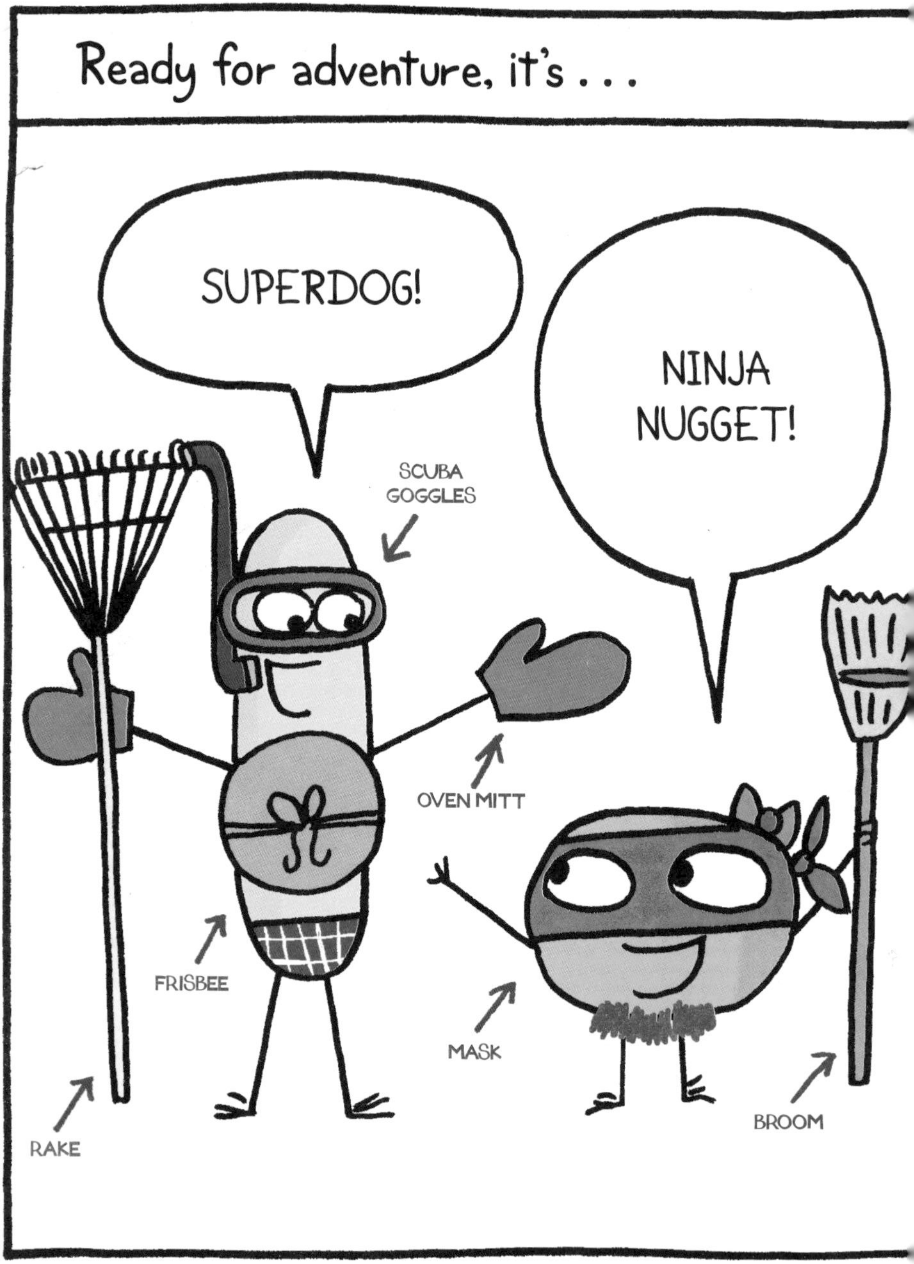
Ready for adventure, it's . . .
SUPERDOG!
NINJA NUGGET!
SCUBA GOGGLES
OVEN MITT
FRISBEE
MASK
RAKE
BROOM

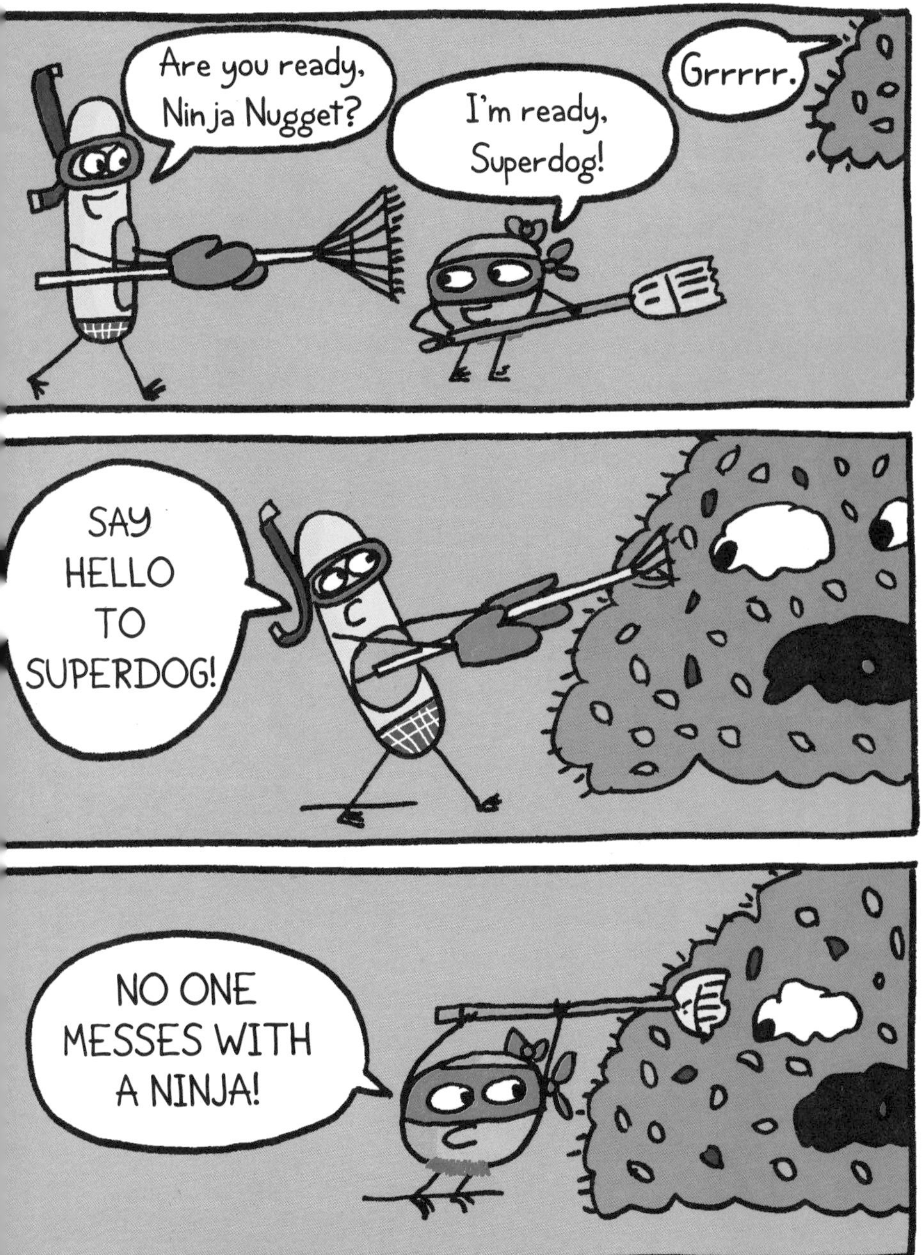
Are you ready, Ninja Nugget?
I'm ready, Superdog!
Grrrrr.
SAY HELLO TO SUPERDOG!
NO ONE MESSES WITH A NINJA!

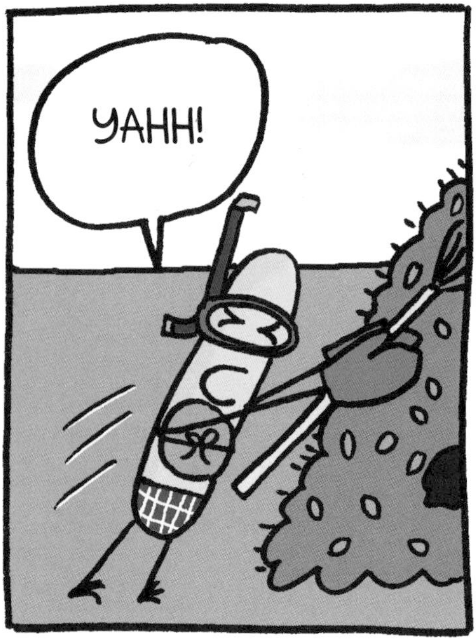
YAHH!
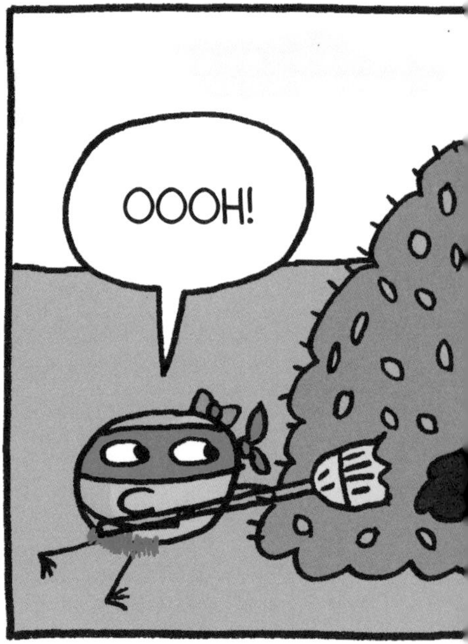
OOOH!
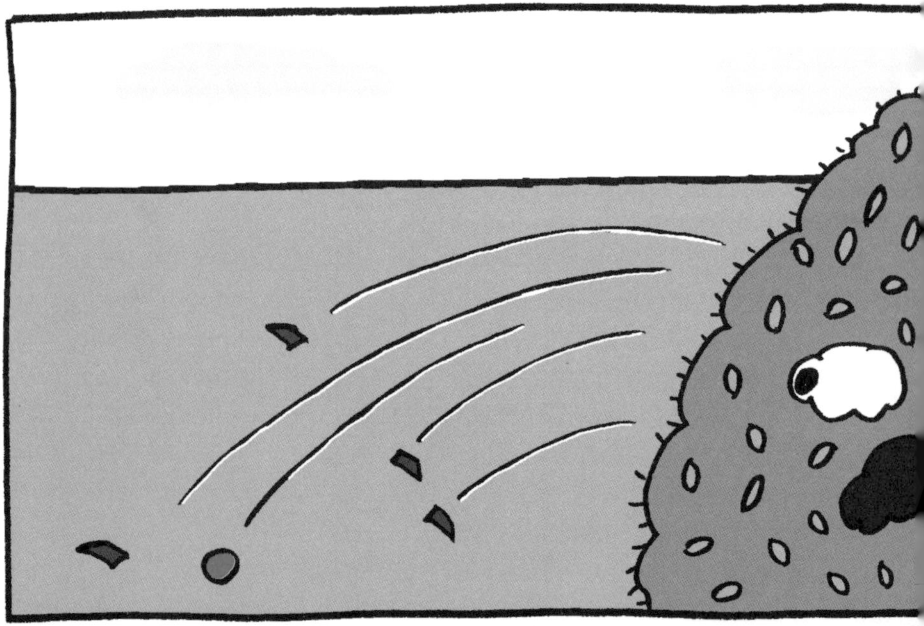

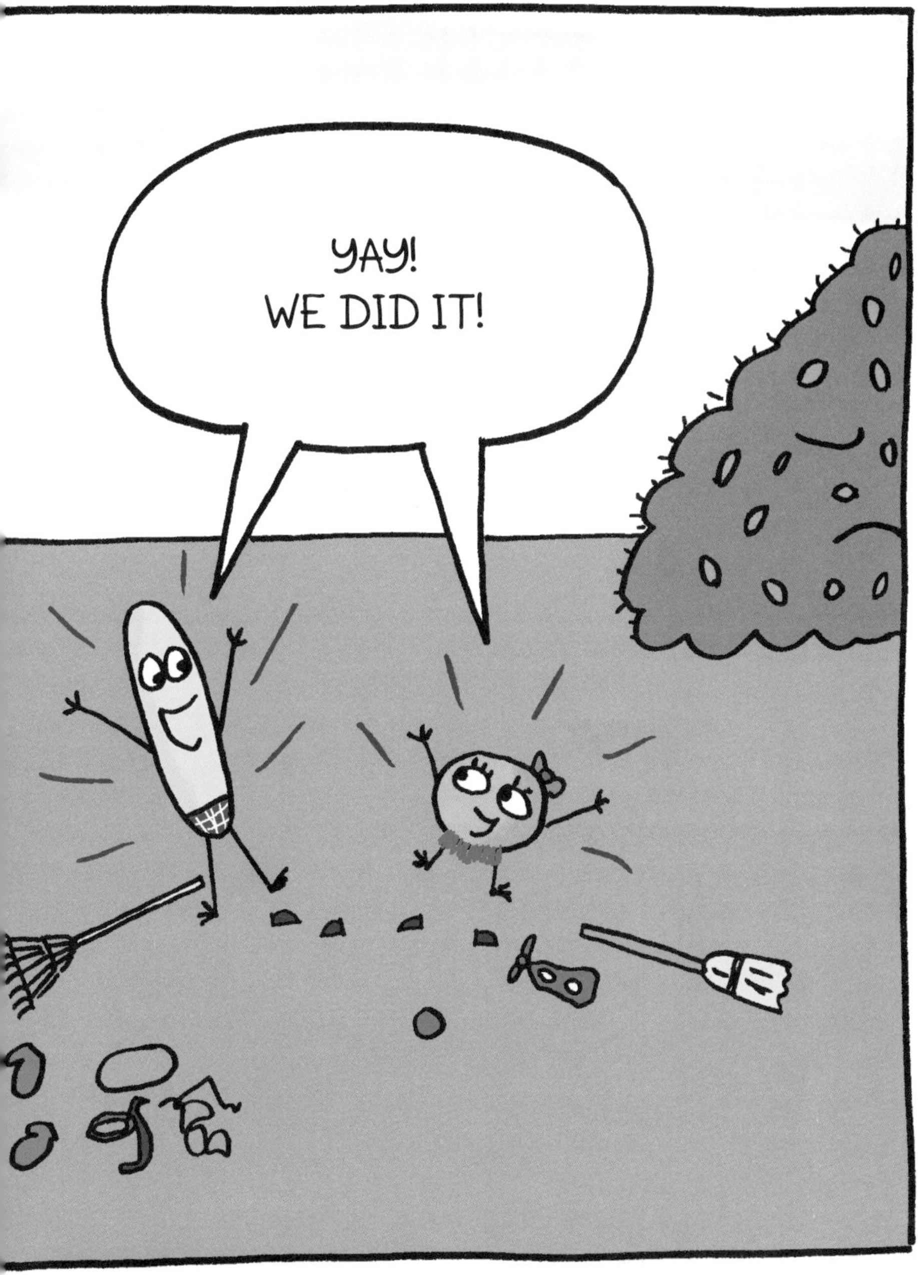
YAY!
WE DID IT!

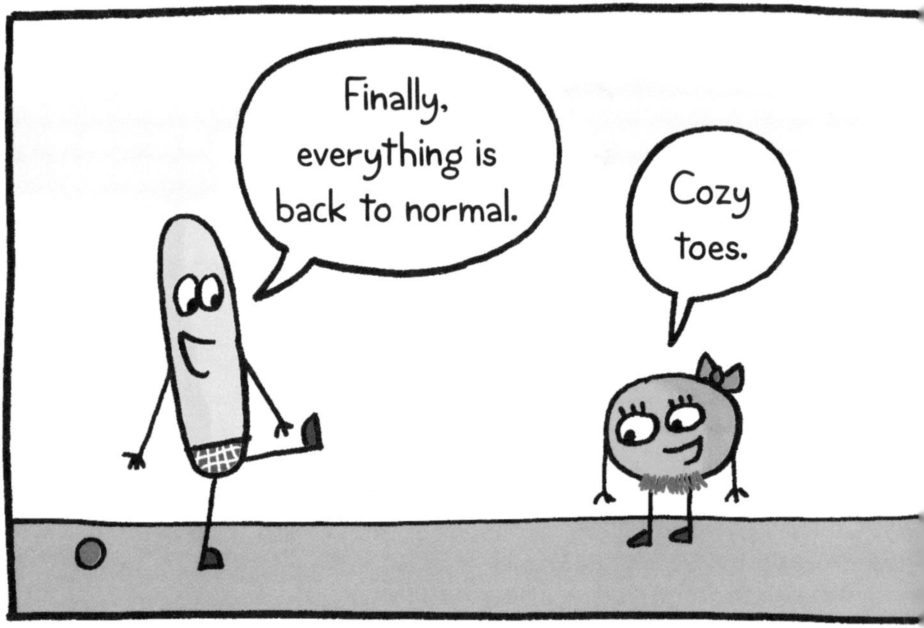
Finally, everything is back to normal.
Cozy toes.

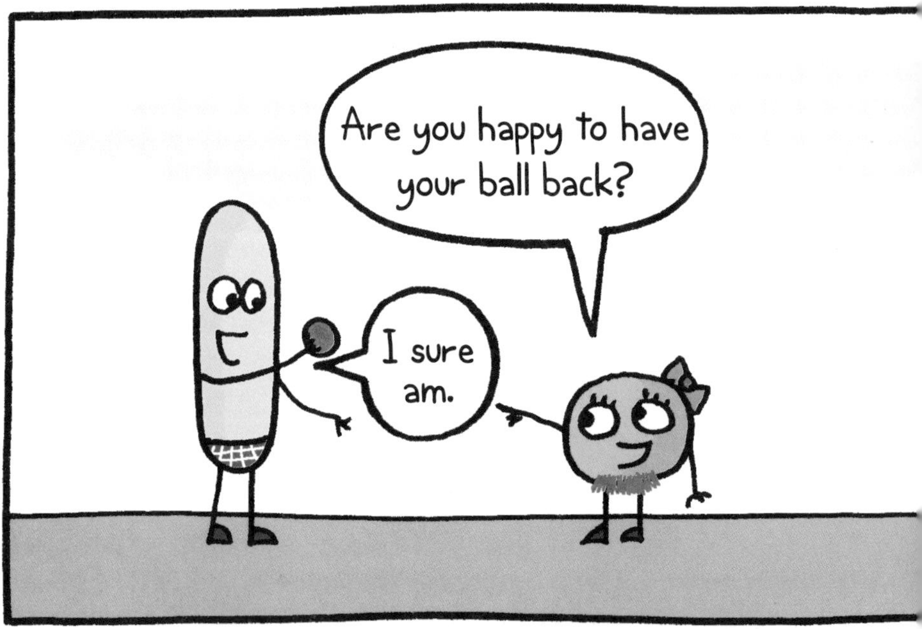
Are you happy to have your ball back?
I sure am.

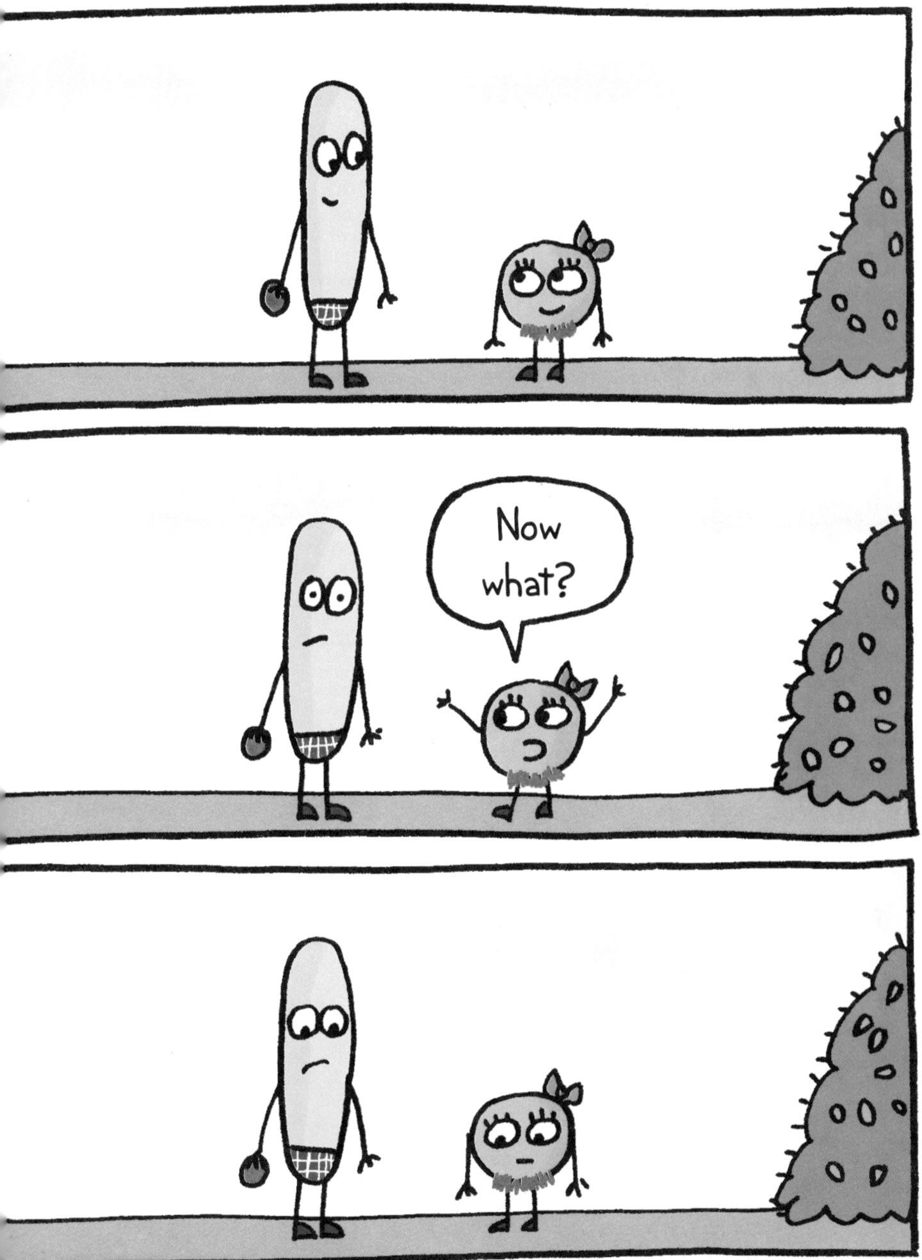
Now what?

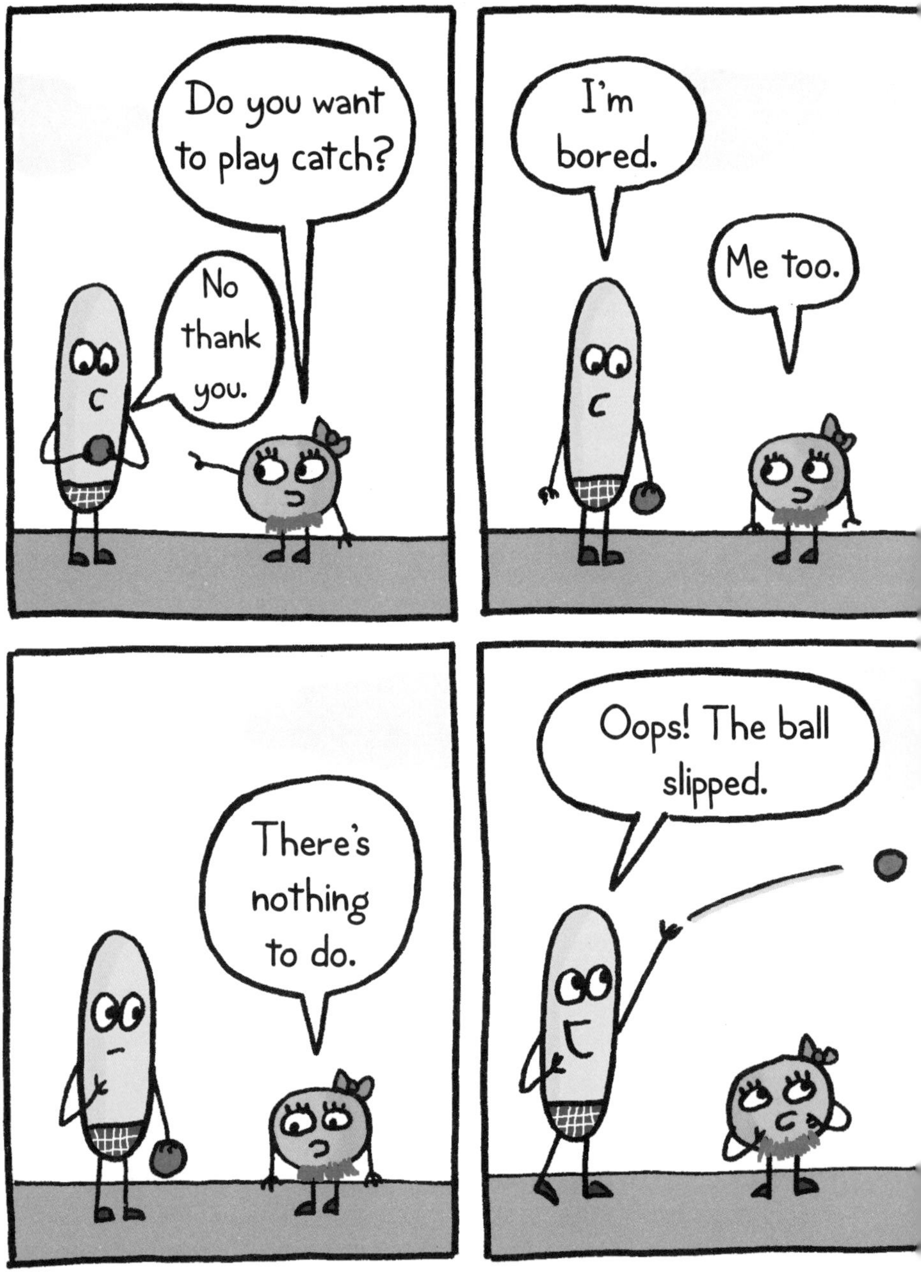
Do you want to play catch?
No thank you.
I'm bored.
Me too.
There's nothing to do.
Oops! The ball slipped.

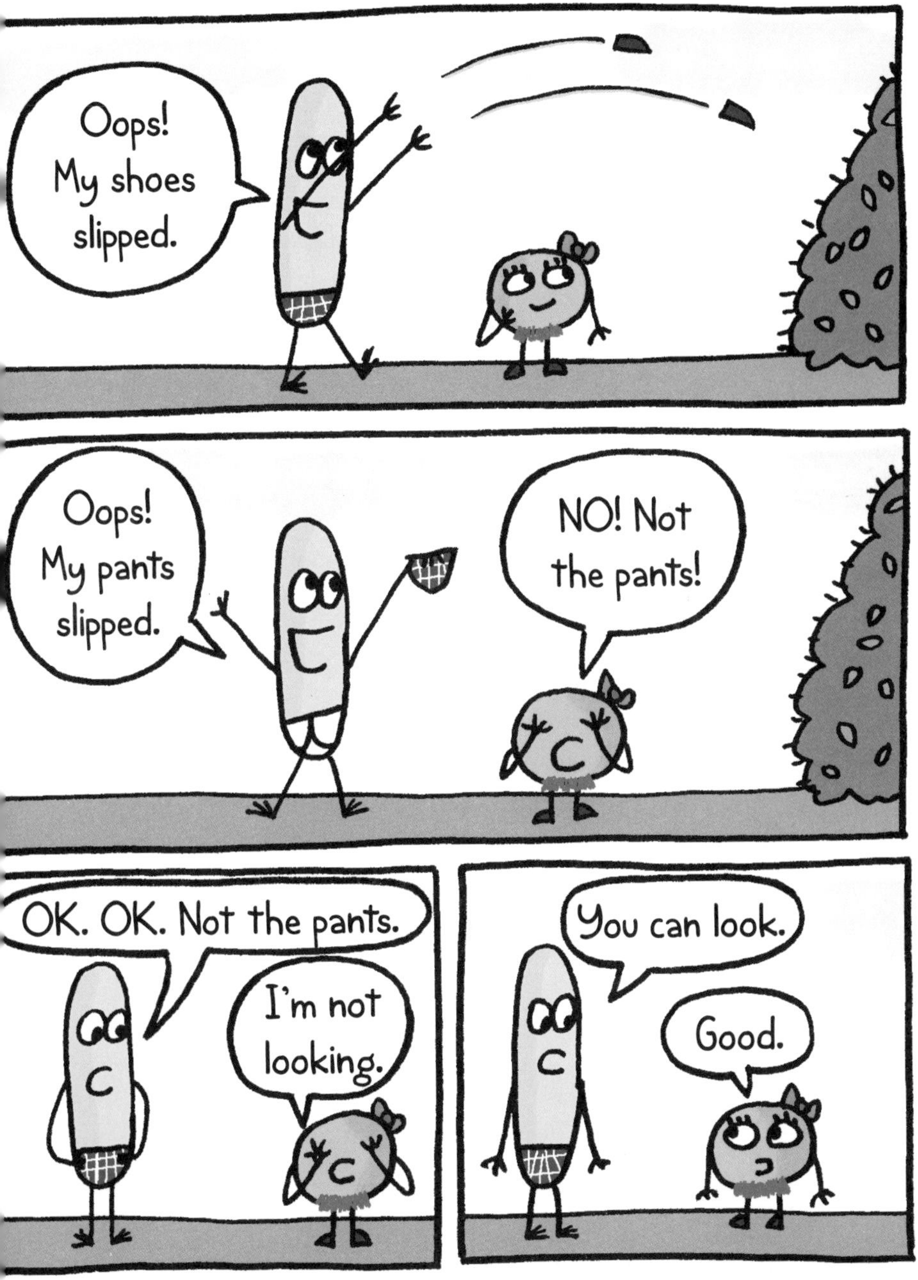
Oops! My shoes slipped.
Oops! My pants slipped.
NO! Not the pants!
OK. OK. Not the pants.
I'm not looking.
You can look.
Good.

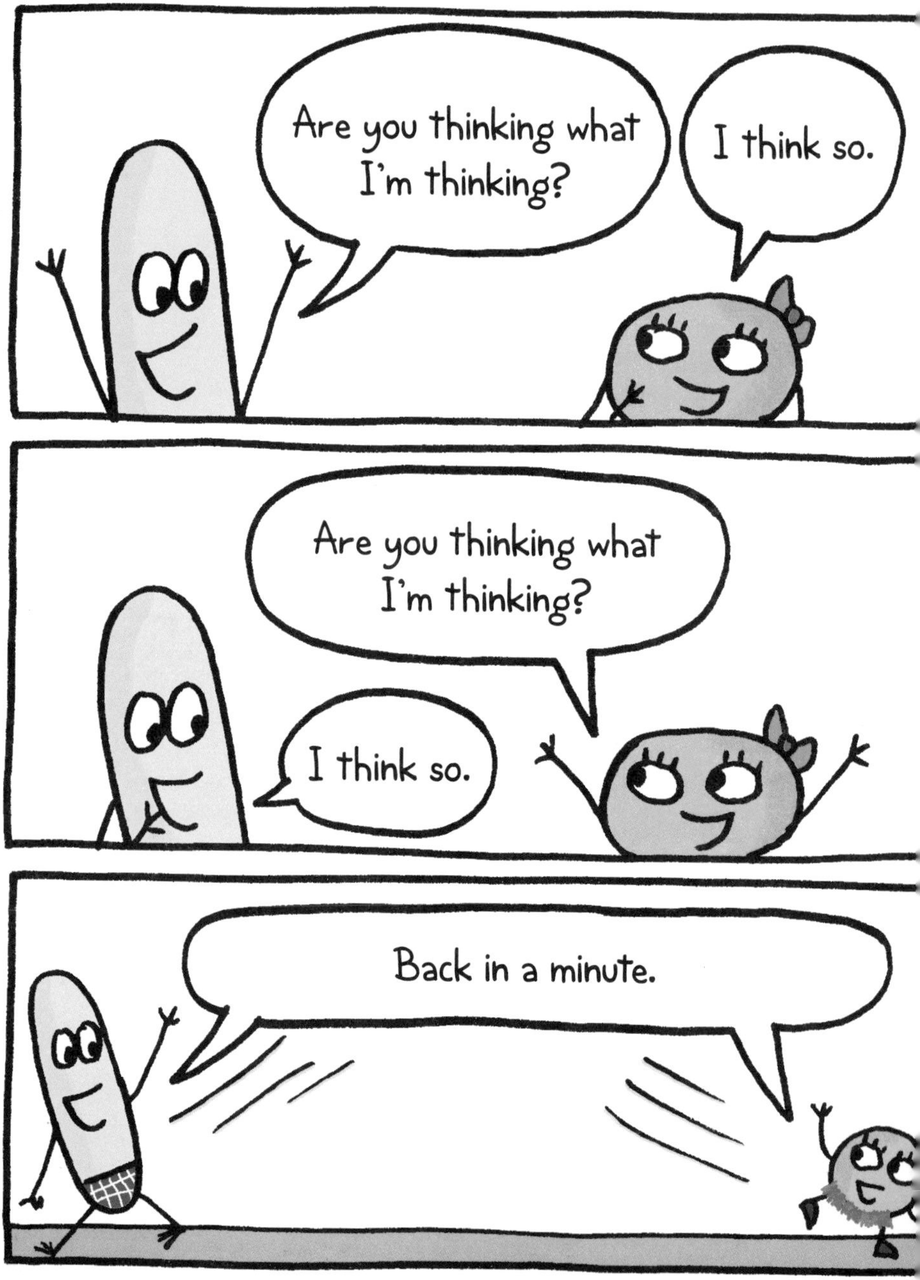
Are you thinking what I'm thinking?
I think so.
Are you thinking what I'm thinking?
I think so.
Back in a minute.

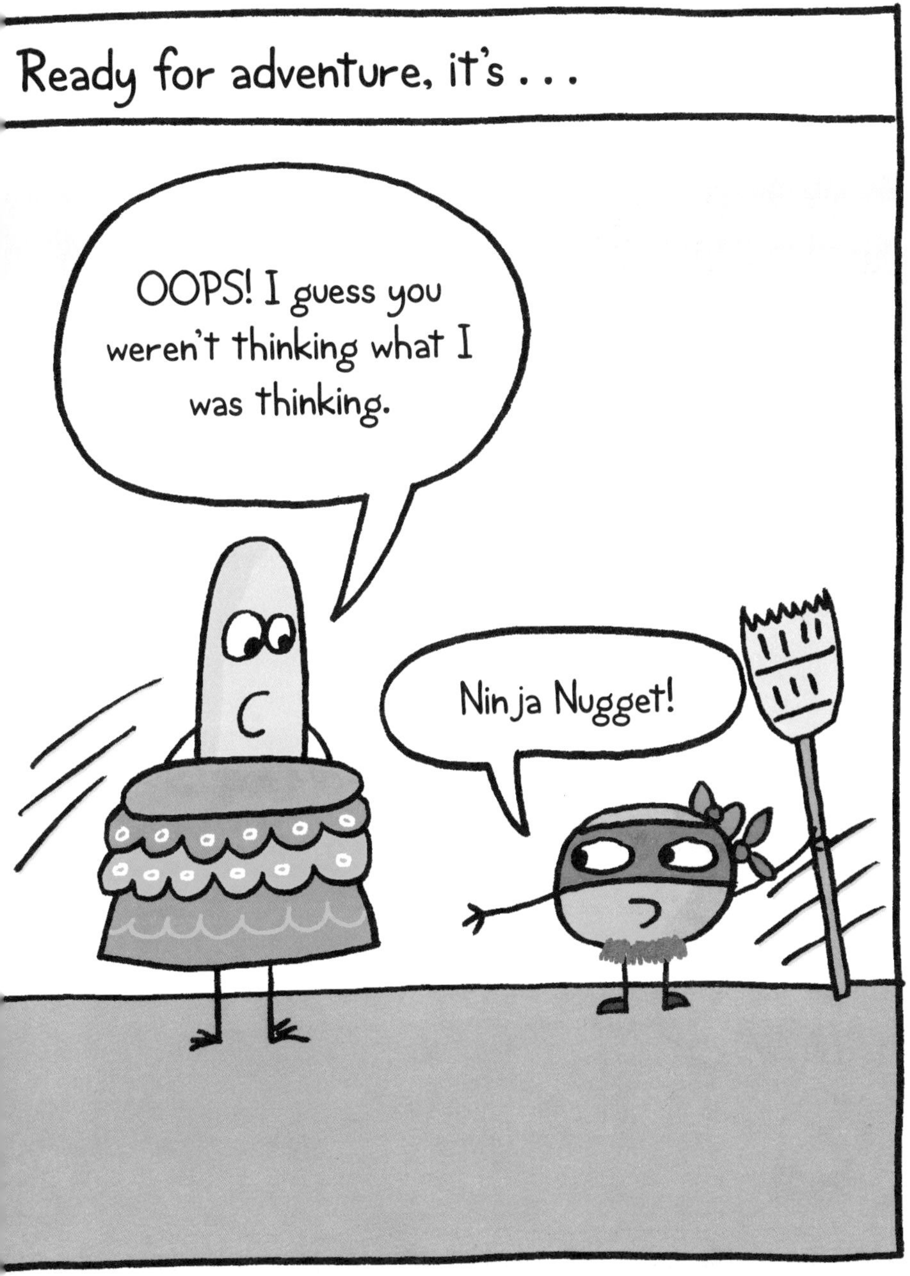
Ready for adventure, it's . . .
OOPS! I guess you weren't thinking what I was thinking.
Ninja Nugget!

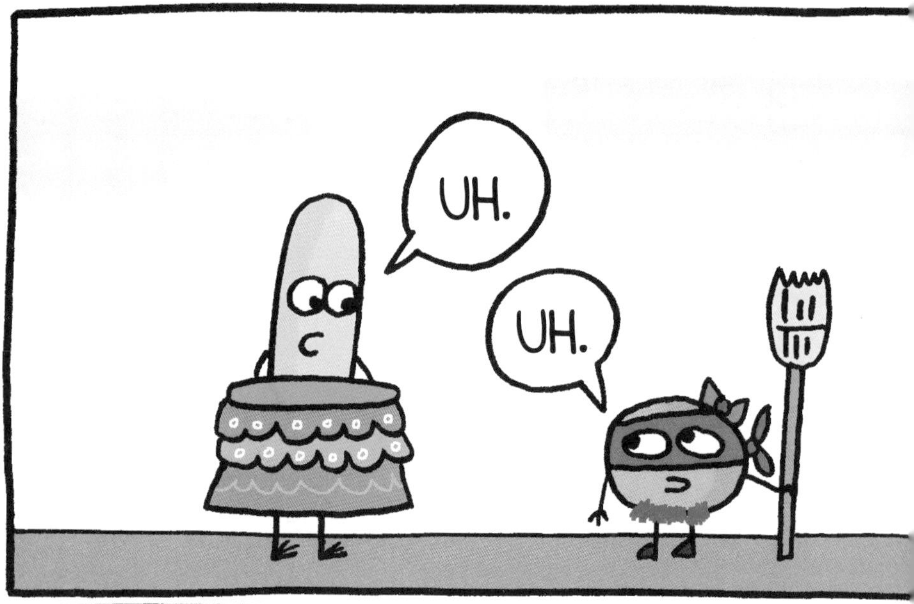
UH.
UH.

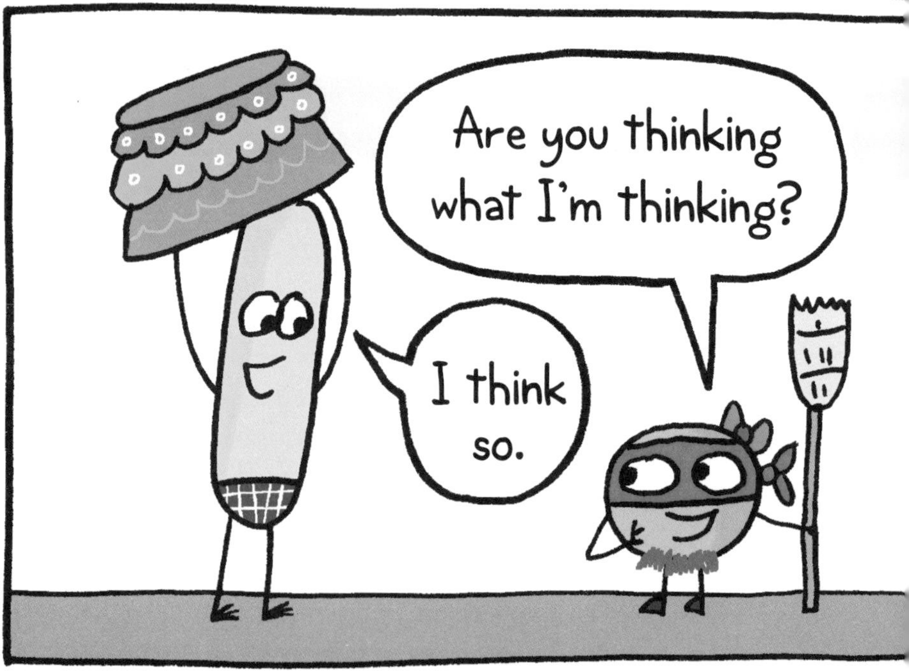
Are you thinking what I'm thinking?
I think so.

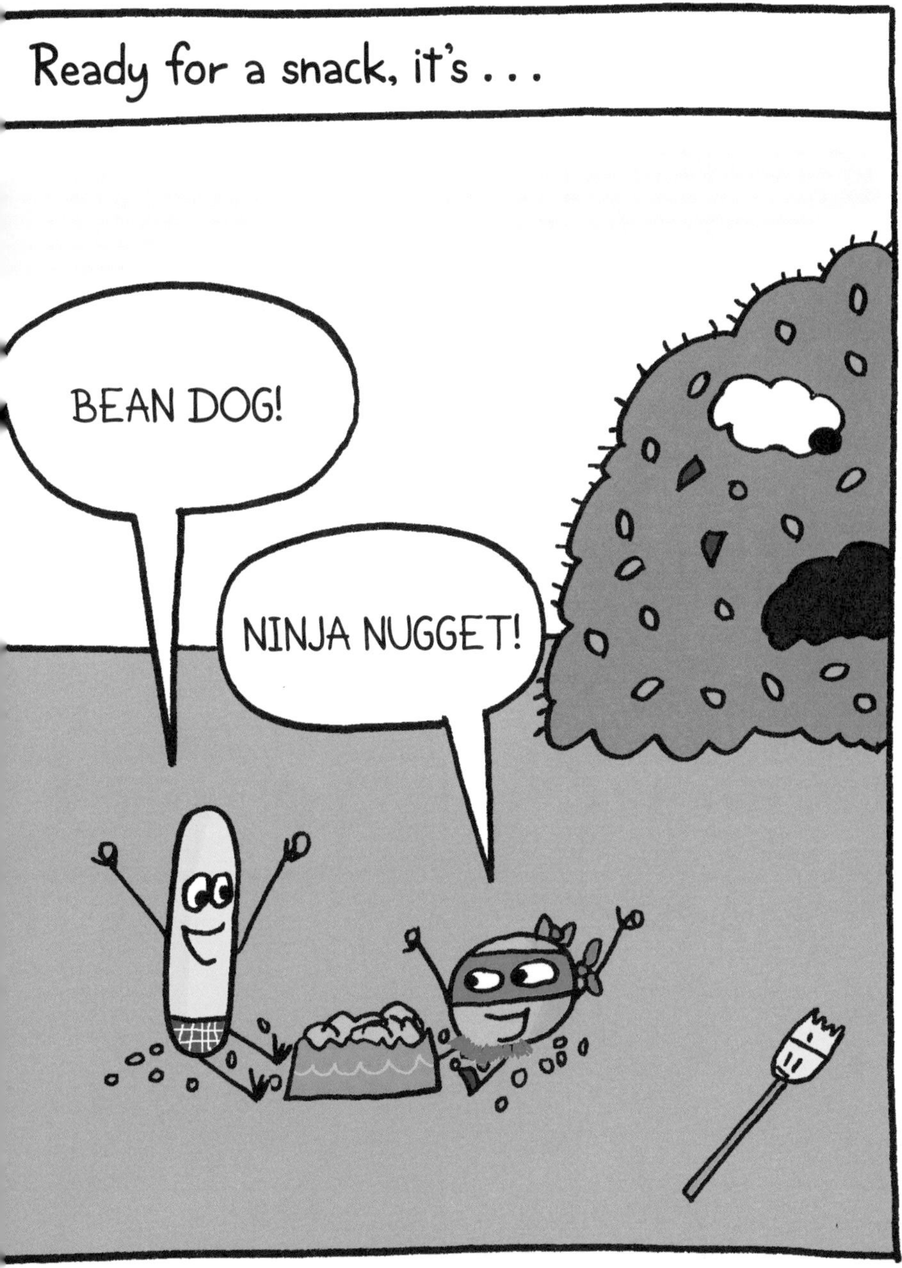
Ready for a snack, it's . . .
BEAN DOG!
NINJA NUGGET!

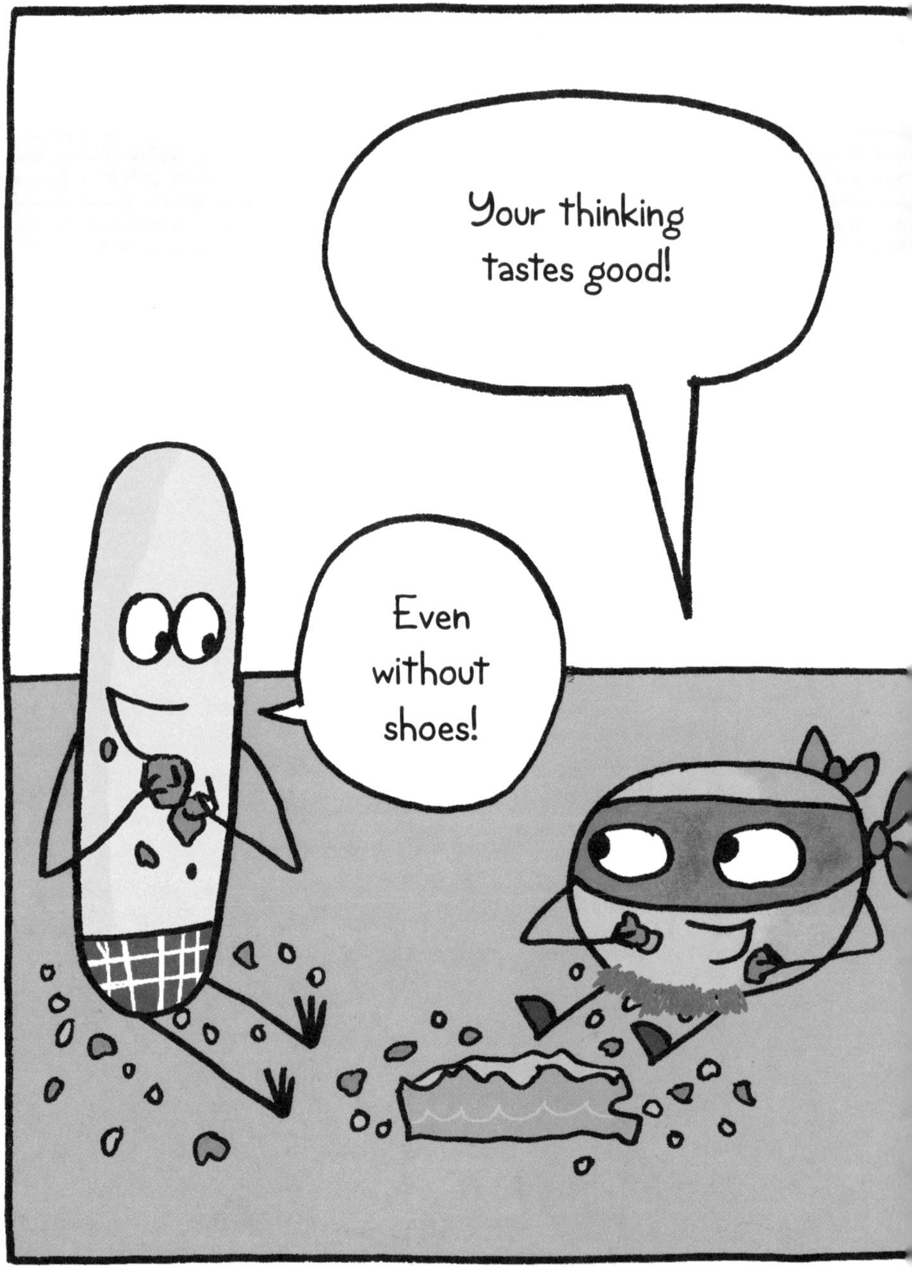
Your thinking tastes good!
Even without shoes!

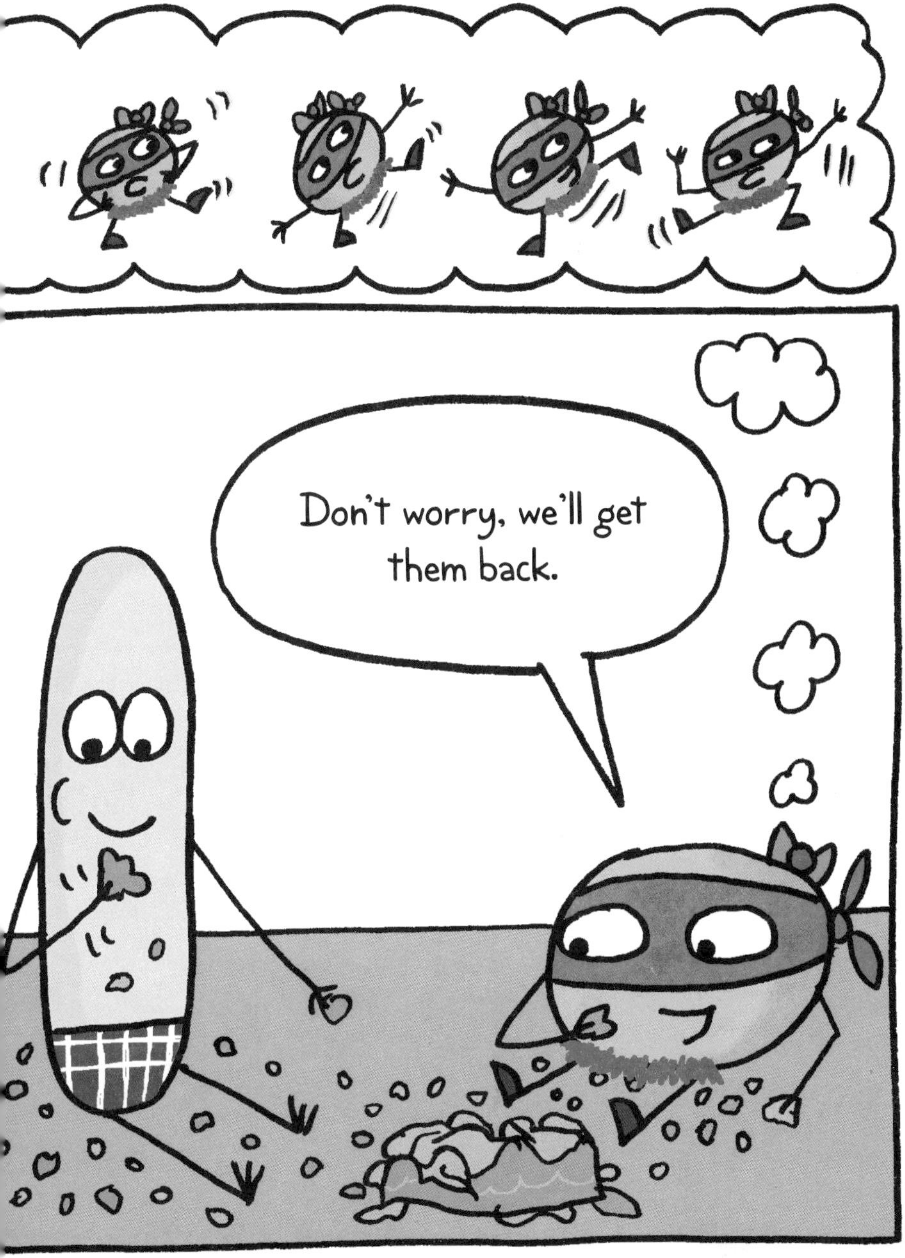
Don't worry, we'll get them back.

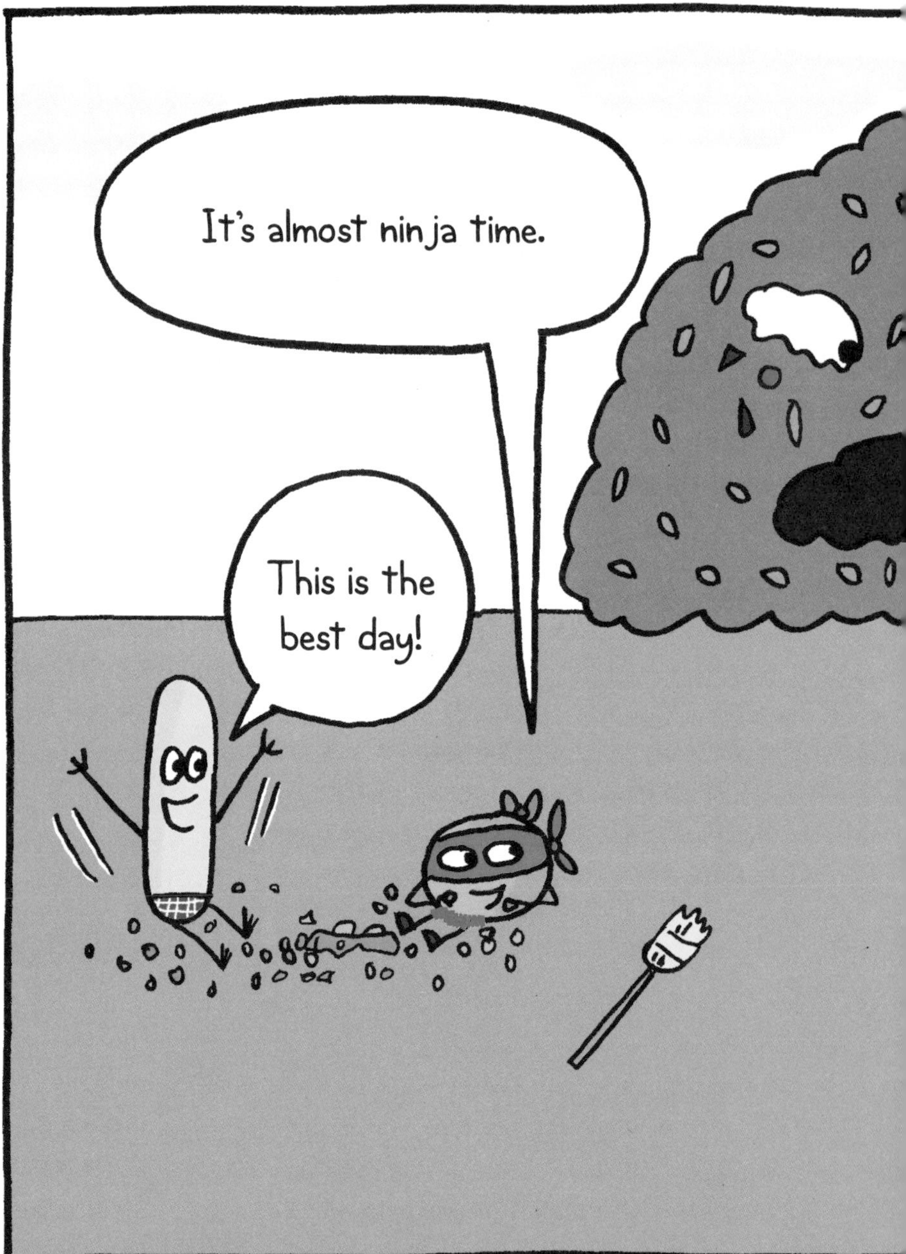
It's almost ninja time.
This is the best day!